Captain Pete

Second Edition

B. Holland Heck

Captain Pete

ISBN: 978-1-961485-88-4 Hardback
ISBN: 978-1-961485-89-1 Paperback

Copyright ©2025 Pan Isles, inc.

First Edition Published in 1967

FV-15

All rights reserved. No part of this book may be reproduced in any form without written permission from the publisher, except for brief passages included in a review appearing in a newspaper or magazine.

Printed in the United States of America.

Published by
Intellect Publishing, LLC
www.IntellectPublishing.com

Captain Pete

To Jack, my husband

By the same author

THE YEAR AT BOGGY
CACTUS KEVIN
THE HOPEFUL YEARS
MILLIE

Captain Pete

Captain Pete

Introduction

In the summer of 1966 Bessie Holland Heck took our family's ferry out to Ship Island. During the 70-minute cruise she met my father, Captain Peter Matthew Skrmetta. She, like many passengers spoke to Captain Pete through the open windows of the pilot house during the trip to and from the island. She was interested in the history of the Skrmetta family boat business and Pete was happy to share a few stories about life on the Mississippi Gulf Coast. As a result of this brief conversation, she became enthusiastic about writing a story in which his boat and Ship Island figured prominently. He agreed and from this chance meeting blossomed the book you're holding.

In 1926, my grandfather, Peter Martin Skrmetta, founded what became our island excursion business, and it has been in continuous operation every year since. In fact, the Skrmetta family has provided passage to over a million Ship Island visitors in the ensuing years. Captain Pete's son Peter Matthew (my father) worked as a young deckhand for the company until becoming principal skipper in 1953 after returning from military service in the Korean War. In turn, I worked as a deckhand and eventually became a third generation Skrmetta boat captain in 1976.

Captain Pete

Of course, the tale within is fiction. Birthed from a creative writer's imagination, the story based on interviews with my Dad and myself. The locations are real, and to tell the truth, some of the stories may not be too far from fact.

At the end of this book is a short history of our family business and pictures of the real Captain Pete, my Grandfather, my Father Captain Peter II with his four sons, along with a photo of the Pan American Clipper (the boat Bessie rode), and of course, Ship Island.

My hope is for you to enjoy this book, and sign up for our next book, the Skrmetta family business memoir which is scheduled to be released for our 100th anniversary in 2026.

Captain Louis Peter Skrmetta

Visit our website: https://msshipisland.com

Captain Pete

Contents

Introduction	page 5
School's Out	Page 11
Aboard the *Clipper Catt*	Page 19
Ship Island	Page 29
Pete Talks to Grandpa	Page 38
A Summer Job	Page 43
Hurricane Weather	Page 54
A Search for Gold	Page 62
The Secret at The Bloody Door	Page 75
Taping Up and Buttoning Down	Page 84
Advice From Sam Tate	Page 96
Back to Ship Island	Page 103
Pete Rescues the *Clipper Catt*	Page 109
Epilogue	Page 118

Captain Pete

Captain Pete

Captain Pete

Captain Pete

School's Out

It was a warm Friday and the early morning sun flooded the carport as Peter Razetta III dashed out to the utility room to gather up his fishing gear. He chose a rod and reel for himself and one for his friend Jim Bob McElroy. Then he put a skillet, a long-handled fork, some plastic plates, and a can of shortening into a tow sack and picked up his swim trunks. His five-year-old twin sisters, Lala and Lenka, were watching him.

"Are you and Grandpa and Jim Bob having a picnic today?" Lala asked.

"Right." Pete stuffed his swim trunks into the tow sack and tied the top.

"Breakfast, children," Mom called from the kitchen door.

Pete left his gear in the carport and went in to breakfast. The smell of bacon and hot cinnamon rolls filled the kitchen. He dampened his hands at the kitchen sink, wiped them on a paper towel, and took his place at the table.

Dad laid his newspaper aside, saying, "I see by the headlines that the President's really pitching for his antipoverty program."

"Humph!" Grandpa Razetta snorted. His gray beard twitched. "Many a man has become a millionaire by staging his own antipoverty program—not sitting around waiting on a government handout."

Captain Pete

Pete watched out of the corner of his eye as Grandpa buttered a roll, his thin, slightly palsied hands trembling.

"Well, Little Pete, now that school's out, what are you going to do with your time?" Grandpa asked.

Grandpa was the only person who called him "Litle Pete" anymore, and Pete wished he would drop the "Little." He took a swallow of his orange juice and answered, "I'm going out on the *Clipper Catt* every day that I possibly can."

"I hope that isn't often," Dad said, grinning. "I hope the tourist trade will be so heavy this summer that you won't get to go more than once a month. The *Catt* will need a new paint job this fall, and we've got to get started on that savings account for your entrance into the academy."

"But Dad!" Pete groaned. "I promised Jim Bob I'd take him to the island real often." To heck with school, he thought. His parents had been urging him to plan for a career in the merchant marine, but he didn't think very much of the idea. It would take too much schooling and besides, the maritime academy they were talking about sending him to was hundreds of miles away—somewhere in Texas. He liked it right here in Biloxi and Gulfport and out in the Mississippi Sounds. "What color are we going to paint the *Catt*?" he asked, hoping to stop further talk of school.

"The same," Dad answered. "White with royal-blue trim and red lettering."

"And captain's blue deck?" Pete asked.

"Captain's blue deck," answered Dad.

"Someday," Pete said around a mouthful of cinnamon roll, "I aim to own a boat just like the *Catt*."

"Oh, no," Grandpa said quickly. "It'll have to be better. Each generation must improve. Captain Zett's boat is lots better than the one I started with thirty-six years ago and—"

"Thirty-six years ago!" exclaimed Lala and Lenka.

Captain Pete

Grandpa and Grandma Razetta had come to the United States from Yugoslavia and had settled in Biloxi, where Dad had been born. Soon after coming, Grandpa had started taking tourists out to Ship Island, where there was an old fort, a relic of the Civil War. The idea of the tour had caught on rapidly, and soon Grandpa had begun making a trip every day during the tourist season. Dad had practically grown up on the boat. Eventually Dad and Grandpa began making two tours a day. To avoid confusion of names, Grandpa was known as "Skipper Pete" and Dad was known as "Captain Razetta." Gradually part of the letters in Dad's name were dropped and now even Mom called him "Zett." After Grandma's death, when Little Pete was small, Skipper Pete had turned the tourist trade over to Captain Zett. Then four years ago Captain Zett had traded the old boat in on the *Clipper Catt*.

Grandpa's face lighted up with remembering. "Your Grandpa and Grandma Bozavic were among my very first paying passengers. When your mother got big enough to go without them, she went out on my boat nearly every day." He smiled at Mom. "She was such a pretty little thing, and she brought me so much trade that I plumb stopped charging her for the trips."

Dad leaned toward Pete and said in an undertone, "Your mother fell in love with your grandpa's boat and married me so she'd have a good excuse for going out on it so often."

"Oh, Zett," Mom scolded. "You shouldn't tell the children such awful things." But she smiled as she said it.

"If my boat has to be lots better than the *Clipper Catt*," Peete said, "I'll make it ten feet longer and give it a hundred more horsepower."

Grandpa chuckled. "You've got a lot more to learn about boats."

The twins chimed, "And we'll call you 'Captain Pete.'"

Pete's chest swelled with pride until Dad suddenly brought his dreaming down out of the clouds.

"At the rate you're going," Dad said, "it'll be a long time before you'll ever earn the title 'Captain Pete.' You only passed to the sixth grade and it should have been the seventh."

Here we go again, Pete thought resentfully. Always riding me about my grades. "What's grades got to do with it?" he said. "Grandpa was a good skipper, and he didn't even—"

"Pete!" Dad scolded.

"Yes sir." Pete bowed his head.

"Grades have a lot to do with it, Little Pete," Grandpa said. "You've got to have an education if you deal with the public. People may not be out to get you, but unless you can speak proper English some of them'll laugh at you behind your back. And unless you can handle figures and money, they'll cheat you." Grandpa's voice was a bit squeaky, now that he was old.

Pete knew that Grandpa and his family, and many of the other immigrants who had come to Biloxi long ago to work in the fishing industry, had not only faced financial problems but had to overcome a language barrier too. Whenever he thought of this he was filled with renewed admiration for his grandfather.

Mom glanced at the electric clock on the kitchen wall. "You fellows are going to be late if you don't get started."

"Right." Dad drank the rest of his coffee and pushed back from the table just as the telephone rang. "I'll get it," he said.

"That'll be Mrs. McElroy," Lala said.

"Yes," Lenka agreed. "She's afraid James Robert might fall overboard."

"Yes, Mrs. McElroy," Dad said into the telephone, "there are life preservers on the *Clipper Catt*. ... No, Mrs. McElroy. ... Yes, we'll try not to let him get too badly sunburned."

Slapping the side of his face, Pete groaned, "Oh, that woman!"

The McElroys had recently moved to Biloxi from western Oklahoma, and they lived only a block from the Razettas. Jim Bob had never been out on a boat and Pete was looking forward to taking him on this trip to Ship Island. They would go out on the first trip of the *Clipper Catt* and not come back until the last. Grandpa was going along, too, and he would stay on the island with the boys.

"Hey, aren't we going today?" That was Jim Bob calling impatiently through the back screen door.

"Coming, Jim Bob," Pete called, hurriedly finishing his scrambled eggs.

Out in the carport, Jim Bob was clutching his red swim trunks, his upper lip curled nervously over his large front teeth. Jim Bob was what the boys and girls at school called a "brain." He was a year younger than Pete and he would be in the seventh grade when school opened in the fall. Pete had to guard himself to keep from being jealous of Jim Bob, for lately every time Grandpa got really provoked at Pete he would say, "Surely, Little Pete, you're as smart as that skinny little Jim Bob McElroy."

Pete put his gear in the car, then holding the door open, he said, "Hop in." Jim Bob slid across the seat and Pete climbed in after him. Dad and Grandpa got into the front seat.

Backing the car out into the street, Dad said, "Wade Hampton over at Gulfport told me that Dick Nolan might be interested in the job as second mate on the *Catt*." He turned the car and drove toward Back Bay, where Dick Nolan lived in a houseboat.

The young man who had been Dad's second mate last season had been called into military service, leaving Dad shorthanded on the *Catt*.

As they rode along, Pete explained his plans to Jim Bob. "There's a concession stand on Ship Island where we can get drinks—and food, too, if we need it. But I hope we won't have to buy food. I'm taking a skillet and some grease and stuff and I hope we can catch enough fish for lunch."

Glancing up, Jim Bob mumbled, "I don't feel so good. Mother made me eat too much breakfast."

Pete studied his friend, wondering if he was trying to think up some excuse to back out at the last minute. Then he shrugged, turned, and poked his face out the open car window just in time to see Radmilla Nincic, who was sitting on her front porch playing with her white cat. "Hi, Radmilla!" he called.

"Hi, Pete!" Radmilla waved back. "Going to Ship Island?"

"Yes. Wish you could come with us."

Radmilla said something, but they were so far past her that Pete couldn't make it out. She was a year younger than Pete, but they were in the same grade at school and had been friends all their lives.

As Dad turned a corner they saw Sam Tate, the school janitor, plodding along toward Brown's grocery store. Grandpa chuckled "I guess Sam's so used to getting up early that he forgot that school was out."

"No, he told me yesterday that he was going to try to get a job as general handyman at Brown's," Pete said.

Grandpa nodded. "He has to have a job somewhere for the summer and Brown's is a good place to work."

The tires buzzed on the gray street, which had been paved with crushed oyster shells. Pete breathed deeply of the cool, scented air. In among the many varieties of oaks lining the street were camphor trees, catalpas, and longleaf pines, some with not a twig for the first thirty feet or so. Here and there wisteria vines had climbed to the tops of the pine trees and were now spreading their blossoms—some lavender, some white—over the branches like gigantic parasols. Great heads of pink crape myrtle nodded in the breeze, and red, yellow, and white roses bloomed everywhere.

"I've never seen a town with so many trees," Jim Bob exclaimed.

Smiling, Grandpa turned in the front seat. "Seems like the builders have a code here, Jim Bob. When they build a new house they very carefully leave as many of the trees as possible."

As Dad neared Back Bay hundreds of shrimp and oyster boats came into view, many with their nets spread to dry.

"Wow-wee!" Pete exclaimed, slapping Jim Bob's shoulder. "What do you think about a sight like that?"

"Mmm," Jim Bob sighed. "It's a painter's paradise."

"I could feast my tired old eyes on a sight like this the rest of my days," Grandpa said.

"I'll be right back," Dad said, getting out of the car. He walked down a short pier and ducked into a houseboat.

Pete looked about. The city of Biloxi, covering a thumblike peninsula, was bounded on three sides by water. Here along Back Bay the houses were small and had been built on stilts to escape the high tides. Lots of frogs and snakes lived in the waters of Back Bay. Old cars and other junk were strewn about. Pete was glad he didn't live here, but even so, the place held a certain fascination for him.

"Up there two blocks is where Roger and Don live," Pete said.

"Yes, I know," Jim Bob answered. "I've been there."

Roger Horvat was fourteen years old and his brother Don was eleven. Their grandparents had come to Biloxi with the Razettas and the two families had been friends ever since.

"Have you heard of Pirate's Tree?" Pete asked.

"No." Jim Bob answered. "What's that?"

"It's down that way." Pete pointed eastward. "It's a giant oak with a knothole about head high. They say Jean Lafitte used to leave love notes and jewelry in it for his girlfriend."

"Why did he leave them there?" Jim Bob asked. "Why didn't he just take them to her?"

"Because her pa would've shot him."

"Oh." Jim Bob mused. "Who was Jean Lafitte?"

"He was a slave trader and smuggler during the War of 1812, wasn't he, Skipper Pete?" young Pete asked.

"Slave trader, smuggler, patriot, or pirate," Skipper Pete said. "Call him what you wish. According to legend he was all of them."

"An old hermit lives down there by Pirate's Tree now," Pete told Jim Bob. "His name is Josiah Sark and everyone calls him Old Joe Sark. He lives in a shack with an icky-looking red door and he calls his place 'The Bloody Door.' "

"Ugh!" Jim Bob's lip curled back over his large teeth.

"He ties his blood-red boat up to Pirate's Tree," Pete continued, "and always goes out in it alone."

"Could we go visit him sometime?" Jim Bob asked. "I've never seen a real recluse."

"We could hide out somewhere and get a look at him when he comes outside," Pete said. "But he's the only person that ever goes inside The Bloody Door."

Grandpa chuckled. "Boys, he wouldn't be a recluse if he opened his place for social calls."

"No ... I guess you're right," Jim Bob said.

Captain Pete

Aboard the "Clipper Catt"

Dad and Dick Nolan, who was half a head shorter than Dad, stepped outside the houseboat and stood talking at the doorway for a few moments. Then Dad came down the pier, whistling. "Nolan says he'll be happy to take the job, beginning tomorrow," he said, getting into the car. "Wally Price is supposed to be at the harbor to go out with me today."

Dad turned the car around and drove back across town to the coast road and then headed west toward Gulfport. The scenic boulevard was divided by a neat median varying in width according to the lay of the land. At one spot the famous old Biloxi lighthouse stood in the median. Above it the United States' flag and Mississippi state flag rippled in the breeze.

Turning in the front seat, Grandpa said, "Jim Bob, did you know that eight flags have flown over Biloxi?"

"Really? Whose were they?" Jim Bob asked excitedly.

"The French, Spanish, English"—Grandpa counted the flags off on his fingers—"the West Florida Republic, the Mississippi Magnolia, the Confederate States, the United States, and the Mississippi state."

"Wow!" Jim Bob exclaimed "Wish I'd brought my notebook so I could take notes."

Pete scowled at Jim Bob. The very thought of a notebook suggested school, and he certainly didn't want Dad and Grandpa to get started on that subject again.

"Hey! Look at that place yonder," Jim Bob pointed ahead to a large house with wide porches and tall, white columns. "That lawn's as neat as a gnat's whisker."

"That's Beauvoir, the last home of Jefferson Davis, who was President of the Confederate States during the Civil War," Grandpa told him.

After they'd passed Beauvoir, Jim Bob turned and looked out across the beach. "That sea wall is so low that I wouldn't have known there was a wall if Daddy hadn't told me the first time we drove along here."

"It's higher from the other side," Pete explained. "And it has steps leading down to the beach. The water never gets up to the sea wall—except during a bad storm or a hurricane."

"I think I'd be afraid of a hurricane," Jim Bob said.

At Gulfport, Dad turned off the highway, drove out to the small-craft harbor, and parked the car. People were milling about the dock, and Grandpa hurried to the ticket booth and began selling tickets.

Wally Price, a sandy-haired, deeply tanned youth, met Dad as he came down the pier. "Good morning, Captain Zett."

"Hi, mate," Dad greeted him. "Are you about ready to go?"

"Aye, sir," Wally said.

Pete stood by the car, admiring the *Catt* sitting serenely on the water—sort of basking in the morning sun. She was a double-decked boat, white with royal blue trim. The words CLIPPER CATT, made of two-foot-high red letters, had been cut from plywood and fastened to the upper rail on either side of the boat.

Ducking back into the car, Pete gathered rods and reeks in one hand and the tow sack in the other. Jim Bob was still huddled in his corner of the seat.

"Well, come on," Pete said.

"I'm not sure I feel like going." Jim Bob's nose twitched. "What if I get sick on the boat?"

"You can hang your head over the taffrail and feed the fish." Pete laughed. "Now come on and help me carry these things."

The boys gathered up their gear and went down to the boat. Dad stood at the gate, assisting the passengers on board. He took Jim Bob's hand, but Pete skipped on by himself. He would have bounded over the rail, but Dad was very strict about safety rules, especially when tourists were about. Leaving their gear in the galley, the boys went up the narrow steps to the upper deck. The *Catt* was the only sight-seeing boat in the harbor, but the water was full of pleasure craft of all sizes and shapes, and over at the Coast Guard station was the brilliant white cutter *Point Estero*.

Pete was proud of the *Catt*. She needed new paint, but even so she was the neatest boat in the harbor, except for the Coast Guard cutter. Dad usually did all the repair work and painting on the *Catt* during the off-season, but last winter he had been so busy at his wintertime job of fishing that he hadn't gotten around to the painting.

With Jim Bob at his heels, Pete turned and walked across the deck. He would have run except that Dad has posted signs which read PLEASE DON'T RUN ON THE BOAT. There was Grandpa, halfway down the pier, bringing up the end of the line.

"Ahoy, Skipper Pete!" Pete called, waving wildly.

Grandpa waved back.

"We seem awfully high," Jim Bob said timidly. "But I guess if we were down below we'd be awfully close to the water."

"I'll take you all over the boat before we get to the island," Pete promised. "Then you'll get used to it."

Captain Pete

With a long blast on the whistle, the *Clipper Catt* cast off. Jim Bob grabbed the rail and his blue eyes grew wide. "We're moving."

"Well, you didn't think we were going to sit here all day, did you?" Pete teased.

The boat rocked a little and Jim Bob hurried to the long center bench running fore and aft of the boat. He sat down and clutched the edge of it.

Pete smiled. "You'll not want to stay there long. When we get a little way out and the porpoises start following the boat you'll want to go down below and see them."

A girl with straight blond hair blowing lightly about her face appeared at Pete's elbow. "Do you mean porpoises really follow the boat?" she asked.

"Well, actually, they lead the boat," Pete explained. "They swim alongside, slightly ahead of it."

"Oh, I sure want to see them," the girl said.

"It'll be a while yet before we're out far enough," Pete told her. He called, "Hey, Jim Bob, we're in the sound now. Over there to the west is Cat Island. Ship Island is almost due south of Biloxi and Horn Island is over to the east. This side of the islands is called the Mississippi Sound, and beyond it's the Gulf of Mexico."

"But what about the porpoises," the blond girl interrupted. "How big are they?"

Other tourists looked at Pete, waiting for him to answer the girl's question.

"They're pretty big," he said. "Six to eight, maybe sometimes ten feet long."

"Where should we stand to see them best?" the girl asked.

"Down in the bow," Pete explained. "You have to hang over the rail and look straight down."

"Where is the bow?" she asked timidly.

Pointing forward and downward, Pete said, "Down there. If you'll watch out to the sides of the boat you'll see a fin—about as wide as your two hands—come up above water. Then just seconds later the porpoise will be alongside the boat."

Pete looked at Jim Bob. "Man, you'll never develop sea legs sitting there. Come on over and join us."

"Look!" cried the girl. "I saw one of the black fins. Let's go down!"

Pete and Jim Bob followed her down the steps to the lower deck. The bow was full of people and the girl looked pleadingly at Pete.

"Push your way through till you get to the rail so you can look straight down," he told her.

She smiled and began doing just that.

Pete turned to Jim Bob. "Let's go back up. We can watch porpoises some other time."

Back again on the upper deck, Jim Bob clutched the rail with both hands and stood rigid against the gentle swaying of the boat.

"Relax, Jim Bob, and don't stand so stiff-legged. Learn to sway with the boat. You know, like riding a horse."

Jim Bob's weak smile turned into a frown. After a moment he asked, "Is that a tiny island away over yonder?"

Pete shielded his eyes and looked across the brilliant blue water. "No. That's a string of barges with a tug pushing them."

"With them so far away, how do you know?" Jim Bob asked skeptically.

"Well, I just know," Pete declared. "After all, I've seen barges all my life. It's probably a cargo of telephone poles ... and maybe some bagged fertilizer. No telling what all else. It's very likely going from Louisiana to Florida."

"Will we meet them?" Jim Bob asked.

"No. They're going too slow. Of course, the *Catt* might meet them on the way back. But we're not coming back this trip, remember?"

"How fast are we going?"

"About nine knots," Pete answered.

"Look!" Jim Bob cried, pointing starboard. Pete looked in time to see two large porpoise fins break water.

A moment later the crowd in the bow went wild. "Look! Look!" the people cried.

"There's one!"

"Here's two on this side!"

"Oh, fiddle, they're gone."

"Jeepers, Pete, I want to go down and see them," Jim Bob said. "But you have to go with me."

Seeing the blond girl starboard, Pete said, "Let's go down on the port side."

At the foot of the stairs Pete pushed Jim Bob ahead of him and they worked their way into the bow and leaned over the rail. Jim Bob went wild with excitement as two porpoises appeared in the water right below them. After a few moments one disappeared, but the other one turned over, showing his white underside, and appeared to glide effortlessly along.

"Look at him!" Jim Bob cried. "He seems to be laughing and playing."

Pete nodded. "Dad says he thinks they really are playing and that they really do like attention."

The porpoise disappeared, but the boys held their places in the bow. From here they could see Ship Island straight ahead.

"Jim Bob," Pete said in a low voice. "Do you want to know one of my secrets? When I get old enough to have my own boat, I aim to train me a porpoise to follow it all the time."

"You're kidding."

"No, I'm not. Of course, Mom and Dad want me to be an officer in the merchant marine, but I don't want to," Pete declared quietly. "I want my own excursion boat and—"

One of the tourists suddenly pushed between Pete and Jim Bob. "How deep is the water here, sonny?"

Pete straightened up to his full five feet two inches and squared his shoulders. "In the channel it's about five fathoms," he told the man. "Outside the channel it's thirteen feet or so." Pete's biggest argument against pushing himself to make top grades in school was the fact that he could answer so many of the tourists' questions. Why bother about school when all he wanted when he grew up was a boat like the *Catt*? Shucks, he thought fiercely, I might even quit school. Like Dennis Popovic.

The Popovics lived over on Back Bay. Dennis was sixteen, and for years he'd spent most of his time down at the wharf or going trawling with the fishermen for weeks at a time. Pete had never been trawling, but he was sure it was more exciting than school. He had begged to go fishing with Dad during the winter, but Dad and Mom wouldn't let him miss school. Then always the tourist season would open just before school closed and Dad would stop fishing and start the tours to Ship Island.

"Skipper Pete, is that a rusty oil tank yonder on the island?" asked an elderly woman.

"No, ma'am, it's a fort, and it's made of red brick," Grandpa explained. "It looks rusty 'cause we're looking at the shady side of it. It's called Fort Massachusetts."

"What's a fort named Massachusetts doing way down here?" a man wanted to know.

"Some say it was named after a Union general's home state," Skipper Pete said, "and others say it was named for the Federal steamship *Massachusetts* which successfully attacked the fort while it was held by the Confederates during the Civil War."

A number of tourists gathered around Skipper Pete as he explained further. "In the fall of 1861, Ship Island was captured and General Butler of Massachusetts moved into the fort with a garrison of seven thousand Federal soldiers."

"Can we go through the fort?" a man asked.

"Yes, you can tour it for a quarter," Skipper Pete said.

Pete turned to Jim Bob. "We'll go through it too, before we go out on the island for the day. And while we're out on the island I'll tell you a true story that'll make your hair stand on end."

"Tell me now," Jim Bob urged.

Grinning impishly, Pete shook his head. "Not yet. But would you like to see on the chart just where we are?"

"Sure."

The boys went back to the upper deck and stood in the doorway of the pilot house.

"Captain Zett, sir." Pete addressed his father quite formally. "May we come in?"

"Aye."

"Captain Zett, my friend here would like to see on the chart exactly where we are." Pete added, "I could manage the helm while you show him, sir."

"I was afraid of that." Dad grinned. He let Pete take the wheel while he unrolled the blue plastic chart on which the islands, channels, and buoys were clearly marked.

"We're right about here." Dad put his finger down at a point well past midway to Ship Island.

With both hands firmly on the wheel and his shoulders back, Pete glanced at the ship's compass, then looked up and sighted on a distant buoy. The last time he'd been on the boat

Dad had let him dock it, but he knew without asking that Dad wouldn't let him dock it today.

"Can Jim Bob take it awhile?" Pete asked.

"Oh, no! I-I don't think I ought to," Jim Bob stuttered.

"Well, for a guy who's as smart at his books as you are," Pete said, "you sure are timid about some things."

Jim Bob thrust out his chin. "Maybe sometime when there aren't so many people on board."

"Jim Bob's right," Dad said, taking the wheel. "Now scram." As the boys turned to go, Dad added, "Bring me a couple of Cokes."

"Aye, sir." Pete saluted his father.

Down in the galley the boys got four icy soft drinks and a bag of potato chips. Moments later they were standing in the stern of the upper deck, watching the boat's wake and tossing potato chips to the crying gulls. The large white birds flapped their wings and, swooping low, scooped up the bits of food almost before they touched the water.

Pete took a long swallow of his drink. "One of these days, when there aren't any tourists aboard, I aim to persuade Dad to let me take the *Catt* all the way to the island dock her." He looked at Jim Bob and exclaimed, "Hey, you're as white as a sheet!"

Jim Bob leaned over the taffrail and threw up. Pete grabbed him to keep him from falling on the deck. "Jim Bob, what's the matter?"

"Oh," Jim Bob groaned, "That churning water makes me so sick."

"Oh, Jim Bob, surely not that," Pete said. Maybe the sun's too hot up here. Let's get you down below in the shade."

Everyone on the upper deck had crowded around them. The blond girl appeared, and she and Pete helped Jim Bob down below, where he stretched out on a bench.

"How much longer till we get there?" the girl asked anxiously. She fanned Jim Bob with a tissue and mopped his forehead.

"Not long." Pete was glad the girl was helping, and he was also glad it was Jim Bob she was fluttering over instead of him.

Grandpa came with a motion-sickness pill and made Jim Bob take it. "Son, if we'd given you this pill when we first started out this morning," he said kindly, "this wouldn't have happened to you. Now you just stay still and try not to talk. We're almost there."

Captain Pete

SHIP ISLAND

The *Catt* began slowing down and Jim Bob sat up on the bench. "Are we here?" he asked.

"Yes," Pete answered. "How do you feel?"

Jim Bob got to his feet. "Fine, I think." He walked to the rail and looked over.

"Let's wait till the crowd is off the boat, then we'll go," Pete suggested.

"Aye, sir," Jim Bob said brightly.

Pete smiled his approval.

When the tourists were off the boat and going down the long pier, Grandpa came over to the boys. "How do you feel, son?" he asked, laying his hand on Jim Bob's shoulder.

"Fine, Skipper Pete. That was a silly thing I did back there."

"Not at all," Grandpa said, "Lots of folks get sick on a boat."

Pete collected his gear, then he and Grandpa and Jim Bob followed the tourists.

"Folks, go to the concession stand and get your tickets to tour the fort," Grandpa called ahead. "I'll wait for you at the gate."

On the lee side of the island the water was smooth and clear. Jim Bob looked down and said, "Hey, look at the oysters and baby conches down there! Could we wade out and get some to take home?"

"We can't wade here," Pete told him. "It's too deep."

"It doesn't look deep," Jim Bob said.

"Still, clear water never looks deep, Jim Bob," Grandpa cautioned. "But it can fool you. It's way over your head along here."

At the end of the pier they stepped off into the moist white sand of the island and walked to the fort gate.

"Grandpa, I'm going to leave our gear here," Pete said. "Me and Jim Bob'll go on through the fort and we'll be back by the time you get through with the tour."

Grandpa nodded, but Jim Bob said, "No. I don't want to go yet. I want to hear what Skipper Pete has to say about the fort."

"I can tell you all about it as we look through it," Pete insisted. But Jim Bob stood firm.

A crowd gathered and Grandpa started his usual speech, making it sound as exciting as if he had actually lived through all the events he told about.

"For about thirty years, beginning in 1699," Grandpa said, "Ship Island was the harbor for the French exploration and settlement of the Gulf Coast. It might interest you young men to know that the first marriageable girls for the early colonists landed on this very island. In fact, if Ship Island could talk it could tell you tales of romance and war and horror and suffering that would make you laugh and cry and cuss and pray all at the same time."

The tourists crowded closer. Pete was proud of the way his grandfather held the interest of his audience, but he'd hear the story so many times. He gripped Jim Bob's hand and began edging through the gate. But Jim Bob, his lips parted over his large teeth, pulled back.

"I want to hear Skipper Pete," Jim Bob whispered.

"During the Civil War," Grandpa continued, "some four thousand captured Confederates were held here. Many of them took sick and died and were buried out there in the sand." He indicated the whole island with a broad sweep of his arm. "Lots of skeletons have been washed up on the beach through the years, so if you folks stumble over one of them out there, don't get too upset. It'll just be another ghost from the past."

A loud groan rose from the crowd.

"Who tells the tourists all this when your grandfather's not along?" Jim Bob whispered.

"Sometimes Dad tells them a little bit of it and sometimes he just hands out literature for them to read," Pete said. "Come on. Let's go."

The boys ran inside the fort and looked up at the high, red-brick walls. At regular intervals along the semicircular wall were steps leading up to a balcony running the full length of the fort. At the top of each stairway there was a rectangular opening in the thick outside wall. Pete and Jim Bob ran across the grass-covered courtyard and up a flight of steps. They poked their heads into an opening and looked out across the water.

"This fort was designed for forty-eight cannons—one for each of these openings," Pete explained. "But the ones they used in here were small compared to the two giant ones they used on top. All of the small ones are gone now, and only one of the big ones is left up on top."

The boys climbed another flight of steps and came out on top of the wall. Looking down at the water, Jim Bob turned pale and put Pete between himself and the outside edge.

"This thing's dangerous," Jim Bob said. "Why don't they put a handrail around it so people couldn't fall off?"

Pete laughed. "That'd take away all the daring and fun of trying to keep your balance up here when the wind's real high."

Captain Pete

"I don't particularly care for that kind of daring," Jim Bob said, his large teeth showing.

"That's Cat Island over there." Pete pointed westward. "And yonder, at the end of Ship Island, is a deep harbor—safe for all kinds of ships in the very worst storms."

The boys started walking around the top of the wall. They could see from side to side of the narrow island, which was covered with a variety of tall grass now waving in the wind. A ribbon of white sand beach laced its way between the green grass and the rippling blue water.

"The island is about seven miles long," Pete continued. "Way on over yonder—to the east—it's so narrow that a big storm cut it in two several years ago. Grandpa says the whole island used to be covered with timber, but during the Civil War the troops cut the trees down on this end and used them for firewood. Only a few small pines that have sprung up in recent years are on this end now."

"What about those skeletons that wash up out of the sane?" Jim Bob asked. "Is that really true?"

"According to history it's true." Pete grinned. "That's why I kept trying to get you to leave while Grandpa was talking. I wanted to tell you that story myself."

"Yes, I know you," Jim Bob said. "You wanted to scare me."

They were nearing the ancient cannon and Jim Bob ran ahead to examine it. Pete looked toward the old lighthouse that stood on the lee side of the island, a mile or so east of the fort. Then he looked southward across the vast expanse of the Gulf of Mexico, reaching on out to the horizon.

Proudly he looked back at the *Clipper Catt*. "Someday I'll own a boat too," he promised himself. "Dad'll be Captain Zett and I'll be Captain Pete and we'll bring twice as many people to the island. My boat just might have a glass bottom so the tourists can see the sea life. And I'll make my tour to *all* the islands and ..."

"Hey, you looking at a ghost or something?" Jim Bob jerked Pete back to the present.

"No, I'm not looking at a ghost or something," Pete said gruffly. He wanted to add, "A fellow can dream, can't he?" but he didn't. Jim Bob would only ask more questions and Pete wasn't ready to tell anybody, except maybe Dad, about his dream.

Grandpa must have finished his talk, because the tourists were now surging into the courtyard and up the steps. The boys went down a dark, dank stairway, crossed the courtyard, and went out the gate where Pete collected his gear. Skipper Pete was waiting for them at the bathhouse.

"Are we ready, Grandpa?" Pete called as he and Jim Bob hurried along.

"We're ready." Grandpa picked up the insulated picnic basket. "I've got us plenty oof cold drinks."

"Aren't we going to put on our swim trunks in the bathhouse?" Jim Bob asked.

"No," Pete said. "We'll wait till the tourists leave, then we'll put them on out there."

"In the open?" Jim Bob gasped.

"Well, no." Pete grinned. "There's a little pine tree out there about as big around as my arm. You can hide behind it."

Jim Bob took his ribbing good-naturedly and they set off across the island through the knee-high grass. When they reached a scrubby pine tree not far from the edge of the beach Grandpa said, "Here's where we'll make camp. This shade's just about big enough for me, and if you boys catch us a fifty-pound catfish for dinner you won't have to drag him so far. Not much grass here either, so it'll be safe for us to make a fire."

"Can we start fishing right now?" Jim Bob asked impatiently.

"No. First we have to find Grandpa some driftwood for a fire."

"That's right," Grandpa said. "I'm wheezing like a tired old horse and I aim to sit right here in the shade and rest." Pete stood looking at the white-capped waves washing in and out. Their swishing rhythm was music to him. He loved the sea and as he looked out across the unbroken distance, he vowed that someday he'd see for himself what was out there.

"Well, let's get the wood," Jim Bob said.

Searching along where the beach met the grass, the boys gathered armloads of driftwood. As they turned back toward camp, they heard a blast from the *Clipper Catt's* whistle.

"What's that for?" Jim Bob asked.

"Dad's warning the tourists that it's time to start back," Pete explained.

The boys tossed their wood down near the pine tree and looked about. Seeing no one, they slipped out of their clothes and into their swim trunks.

"Boy, are you ever white!" Pete teased, comparing his own husky, brown body to Jim Bob's pinkish-white one.

Captain Pete

"Don't forget that in Oklahoma where I came from you wear lots of clothes all winter," Jim Bob said.

They grabbed their rods and reels and ran for the water.

"Don't go too far out," Grandpa cautioned.

"We won't," Pete called over his shoulder.

They stepped into the water and immediately a cold wave wrapped itself around their legs. Both boys screamed—Pete with delight, Jim Bob with surprise edged with fear.

"Come on," Pete cried.

"How do you know we won't step into a deep hole?"

"Because I've been here before. If we don't go too far out we're quite safe."

"Don't worry," Jim Bob said. "This is as far out as I'm going."

They began casting into the surf and on the third try Jim Bob got a strike and yelled for Pete to help him reel it in. Grandpa came to watch.

"Hey, now, ain't that a dandy," Grandpa praised when Jim Bob held up a catfish.

"How long do you say it is, Skipper Pete? Jim Bob asked.

Grandpa spanned the fish. "Sixteen inches."

"Wow!" Jim Bob exclaimed. "That's a pretty good-sized fish, isn't it?"

"It sure is," Grandpa said.

Pete had hoped he'd catch the first fish, but he tried not to show it. He waded back out and cast again. Something struck his line and he began reeling it in.

"I've got one!" he yelled. "He's a big one and he sure is a fighter." The fish jumped high out of the water and Pete cried, "A trout! Grandpa, I've got a trout!"

Forgetting his fears, Jim Bob ran out to Pete, babbling wildly. Pete brought the thrashing trout to land. "The way that thing fought," he said slowly, "I figured he was lots bigger."

Captain Pete

"He's a pretty good trout at that," Grandpa said.

When the boys had caught nine fish, Grandpa told them to stop. "This is more than we can eat, boys. You rest while I fry them. And, Jim Bob, you better put your shirt on or you'll blister and your ma won't be happy with us."

Pulling his shirt on, Jim Bob ran back to the beach and began digging in the sand. Pete sat down with his back against the pine tree, muttering to himself. "How come a landlubber, who's probably never been fishing a dozen times in his whole life, caught more fish than me?"

"Hey, Pete, come on!" Jim Bob called. "It's lots of fun."

Captain Pete

Pete only waved. But he couldn't stay glum for long; it was good to see his friend happy. After a while he said, "Grandpa, Jim Bob's a good fisherman, isn't he?"

"Jim Bob's good at a lot of things, Little Pete," Grandpa said. "He probably learns more from books in one month than you learn from experience in a year."

PETE TALKS TO GRANDPA

Pete helped Grandpa prepare lunch and when it was ready he called, "Hey, Jim Bob, let's eat."

Jim Bob splashed into the water and washed the sand off himself, then galloped to the campsite. "Man, this is the life!" he exclaimed.

Grandpa chuckled as he and the boys sat down in the shade of the little pine tree and began picking off sufficient bits of fried fish, all brown and crispy on the outside and white and flaky on the inside.

"Just to be real honest," Jim Bob said around a mouthful o bread and fish, "I didn't think I'd like the sea. But I'm about to change my mind."

"You mean you might want to own a boat of your own—like me—someday?" Pete asked.

"Oh, no, not that," Jim Bob said quickly. "I'm going to be a newspaper reporter, and someday I'm going to write a book."

Grandpa looked admiringly at Jim Bob. "Say now, that's what I call good planning—decide early in life what you want to be, then go after it."

Pete scowled and looked the other way. He already knew what he wanted to be—captain of his own boat, just like Dad. But instead of his family encouraging him in that direction, they wanted to send him off to some stuffy old academy. It isn't fair, he thought resentfully.

"Right here on this island would be a good place to set a mystery story," Jim Bob was saying. "I can just see the title now: *Peg-leg Pirate Buries Chest of Gold.*"

Grandpa smiled. "Better think up something more original than that, Jim Bob. That one's been done to death."

"Well then," Jim Bob said confidently, "I'll just turn it over to my subconscious mind and we'll come up with something."

Pete squinted at Jim Bob. "Sometimes I think you talk like a nut."

Grandpa and Jim Bob laughed, but Pete didn't see anything particularly funny.

After they finished lunch, Jim Bob ran back out onto the beach. "Hey," he called. "This hole I dug is half full of water."

Pete waved at him.

"That boy's really having him a time," Grandpa said.

Pete began helping Grandpa clean up the campsite. "Grandpa," he said slowly, "about this morning at the breakfast table. All I started to say was that you never finished school and you made the best skipper in the whole Gulf of Mexico. But the way Dad interrupted me made it sound like I meant to say you never even went to school."

"Now don't you go fretting yourself about that, Little Pete. I know what you meant. You and me, we understand each other."

Pete put the forks and plastic plates in the tow sack with the skillet and sat down in the shade. Grandpa covered the dying fire with sand then he sat down and leaned back against the tree. "Little Pete," he began seriously, "when I came to this country I adopted it all the way. And I set myself to know its history—"

"I reckon nobody knows more history than you do," Pete interrupted.

"That isn't the point I started to make. What I started to say was, times are different now. Any more, you've got to have an education to get a good job."

"But, Grandpa, I only want my own boat," Pete flared. "And I know all about running the *Catt*."

"Hold on there, boy," Grandpa said sternly. "These days the law says a young'un has to go to school."

"The Popovic and Horvat kids don't go. Only once in a while."

"That's because the law isn't enforced here as strictly as it ought to be," Grandpa said. "But, son, it isn't wise to compare ourselves with others. We should do the best we can with our own talents, regardless of what the other fellow does." After a moment he continued. "Sometimes, Little Pete, we have to bend with the wind to keep from being broken."

"But, Grandpa, is that fair? I mean, that somebody should make a law that everybody has to follow?"

"Yes, I reckon so. If it's a good law. At any rate, the idea has been around a long time."

"But why can't people be free to do what they want to?"

"Son, I know you're just a boy, and I don't want to expect too much of you. But if you'll just stop and think about it you'll realize there is no freedom without discipline. Why, if we all set out to do just as we pleased, with no thought for the laws of the land, in no time at all people would be like savage beasts and civilization would have to start all over again."

Pete picked up a stick and began gouging holes in the ground. "Grandpa, the other day I asked Dad and Mom if I could have a motorboat for my birthday and they said No, that a twelve-year-old wasn't mature enough to be turned loose with a power-driven boat. But lotsa kids younger than I am have boats."

"Lots of kids have accidents, too, Little Pete," Grandpa said. "I agree with your parents."

"Dad said if I'd start a savings account and save enough for my own down payment that they'd help me buy an outboard when I finish junior high. But, doggone, Grandpa, I'm not even in junior high yet, much less anywhere near finishing."

Grandpa nodded. "In that case, when school starts next fall you'd better buckle down and learn all you can—"

"Grandpa, it isn't that I don't want to learn," Pete interrupted, "I do. I want to learn lots of things, everything. But school is such a waste of time. Criminalities! Nine months out of every year spent in a stuffy ole schoolhouse!" He paused, then continued fiercely, "And you wanna know something? Every time I start thinking about what I really want to do when I grow up, some nosy ole schoolteacher says 'Pete, stop daydreaming and get to studying!'" Pete's breath came fast and his eyelids flickered.

"I understand, son," Grandpa said quietly. "I understand."

"Hey, Pete, come on," Jim Bob yelled. "The summer's a wasting."

Grandpa laid his hand on Pete's shoulder. "Jim Bob's right. Go on and have fun and stop worrying about school."

Pete kicked up a shower of sand with his bare foot. It seemed easy enough today for Grandpa to say forget about school. But Pete couldn't help remembering how the whole family had treated him last night after they'd seen the low grades on his report card.

"Why, Pete!" Mom had sputtered.

Dad had said, "I'm telling you, boy, if you don't make better grades than these next year you're going to summer school every year until you make up a whole grade."

Then Grandpa had said, "I'll bet that skinny little Jim Bob McElroy made better grades than these."

And now, less than twenty-four hours later, Grandpa was saying stop worrying about school. Pete snapped the stick across his knee and got to his feet. He had to figure out a way to make some money so he could start that savings account. He might end up having to buy a boat all by himself.

He turned toward the beach. If he could just find some pirate's gold here on the island … The thought was exciting, but it was a dim hope. There probably wasn't a spadeful of sand on the whole island that hadn't been turned over a dozen times since the days when pirates buried chests of gold. Tomorrow he'd better start looking for a job, he decided, and then he stalked out to where Jim Bob was digging in the sand.

Jim Bob looked up at Pete and asked, "Well, what clouded your face?"

"I think it's a pigment of somebody's imagination that I have to go all the way through high school and on to—" Pete stopped as Jim Bob began rolling with laughter and pounding the wet sand with his fists. "Well, what bit you?" Pete snarled.

"Ha-ha!" Jim Bob suddenly stopped laughing. "The word is 'figment,' not 'pigment.'"

Pete glared down at him. "So what? Figment or pigment. What difference does it make?"

Jim Bob got to his feet. "It makes a lot of difference. The difference between a guy who knows what he's talking about and one who doesn't."

Pete turned away, flushed with embarrassment.

A SUMMER JOB

The morning after his trip to Ship Island, Pete went out to look for lawns to mow. But finding a job was harder than he had imagined. He was about to give up, when his luck suddenly changed and he got two lawns to mow every week. One was small, and he and the woman agreed that two dollars would be fair. The other lawn was larger and he got three dollars for it. When he finished mowing the lawns that morning, he collected his pay. Five dollars seemed like a lot of money, and he whistled gaily as he pedaled home on his bicycle, taking the five crisp one-dollar bills out of his pocket every now and then to look at them.

Feeling that his good fortune called for a celebration, Pete decided to treat Radmilla, Jim Bob, and himself to big, thick malted milks. After paying for the drinks he had only twenty-one cents left out of a whole dollar. He looked at the two dimes and one penny in the palm of his hand, then hurriedly put them in his pocket.

"Oh, well," he said elaborately, "I guess it's worth it."

"It sure is," Jim Bob said. " 'Specially on a day as hot as this."

In the late afternoon Pete began thinking how good a chocolate ice-cream cone would taste. When he went to look for Lala and Lenka to take them to the Tastye Stoppe he found Grandpa dozing in the hammock, so he offered to treat him too.

"Oh, you don't want to spend your hard-earned money on me," Grandpa protested.

"Sure I do," Pete insisted. "What kind do you want? Of course it'll only be ten-cent cones."

"I'll bet you spent more than that on Jim Bob and Radmilla," Lala accused.

"Hold on there, Lala," Grandpa said. "Let's not bite the hand that's feeding us."

At the Tastye Stoppe the twins chose their favorite flavor of ice cream and Pete ordered two vanillas—one for Mom and one for Grandpa. He pushed another of his precious dollar bills through the window and the girl slapped his change down. He picked up one quarter, two dimes, and two pennies. His money was going fast, he thought fearfully.

The children in the neighborhood heard that Pete had money, and on Sunday he spent another $1.57. Leaving his friends out by the swing, he slipped away to his room and spread his money on his dresser.

Only $2.11 left. "I'll never get a boat this way," he groaned.

That night he and Dad got their flashlights and gigs and went floundering. As they drove toward the beach, Pete discussed his money problems with his father.

"I didn't think I was spending very much," he wailed. "But it just seems to melt away."

"I know," Dad said understandingly. "And until you learn to control your money, instead of letting it control you, it won't ever be any different."

"Yes, but how do you do that?" Pete asked lamely.

"It takes practice, son. And patience." They were silent awhile, then Dad added, "You don't want to be a tightwad, but on the other hand, you don't want to be a spendthrift either. And you don't want a bunch of fair-weather friends to get the idea that you're a softy."

Pete had been doing some figuring in his head. "At two dollars aa week, I won't have enough money to buy a boat by the time I'm out of *senior* high."

"Just a minute," Dad said. "You're going at this all wrong. After all, you didn't expect to make enough money mowing lawns to buy a boat. You only intended to start a savings account, remember?"

"I know. But doggone! Only two dollars and eleven cents left out of five dollars."

"Well, the thing for you to do is to hang on to what you have, and the first thing tomorrow morning let your mother take you to the bank and open that savings account. Then on the days when you finish your mowing, go by the bank right then and deposit two dollars."

"Oh, no," Pete said quickly. "I want to deposit at least three dollars and maybe four. Actually, a dollar a week is enough spending money for me."

"It's up to you to decide how much you want to spend and how much you want to save," Dad said. "The important thing is that you set yourself a goal, then work toward it." They had reached the beach and Dad pulled off the highway into a parking area. Lights dotted the water where others were fishing for flounder. "How about us getting out there before the other fellows catch all the flounders?" Dad said.

They waded out into the water and Pete held the light on the flat fish swimming just below the surface of the water while Dad speared them with the gig and put them in the bag. The floundering kept Pete's mind off his troubles, but later that night as he lay in bed with the moonlight shining through the window, he tried again to think of ways to make more money for his bank account.

"I might finish high school," he muttered to himself, "but I sure don't want to go hundreds of miles away from home and study for years just to be an officer in the merchant marine." He pounded his pillow and finally went to sleep.

Several days later Jim Bob came galloping into the Razettas' backyard with a notebook in his hand. He plopped down in the shade beside Pete, who was making a lure with a fishhook and a bright orange feather.

"Pete, we've got to figure out some way to get your father to take us back to Ship Island," Jim Bob said excitedly.

"Why?" Pete began winding a nylon thread around the feather and the hook.

"Because I'm writing a mystery story and setting it on the island and I have to do some research."

"What do you want to know?" Pete asked. "Here, hold this real tight while I tie the thread."

Jim Bob took the eye of the hook between his thumb and forefinger and clamped down. "I want to see exactly where the prisoners slept, so I can get the feel of things."

"They slept on the ground mostly." Pete snipped the nylon thread and held up the lure. "Isn't that a dandy! I'll bet I catch a bass with it."

"Sure," Jim Bob said. "But when do you think your father will take us to the island?"

"Soon I hope. I want to try my new lure."

The boys climbed into the hammock at opposite ends and lolled in the shade.

"Guess what?" Jim Bob said. "I rode my bicycle down by The Bloody Door yesterday and I saw Old Joe Sark come out and lock the door behind him."

"Oh?"

The Bloody Door is sure a good name for that place," Jim Bob observed. "I've never seen such a color."

"Didn't I tell you?"

"He untied his red boat from Pirate's Tree and took off."

"Probably going fishing."

"How does he make his living?"

"He's a World War I veteran," Pete answered. "Dad says he gets a pension."

"Did you ever see him close up?" Jim Bob asked.

"Sure. Many times," Pete said. "He's a little ole dried-up man, not a tooth in his head. Has real black eyes that look right through you."

"That's him all right," Jim Bob said. "I reckon I'll have to write a story about him some day."

Pete sat up, grinning. "For now, let's go visit Roger and Don."

Pete and Jim Bob pedaled their bicycles faster than the hot summer breeze. When they reached the Horvat place the front shades were drawn and they were afraid no one was home. Pete knocked on the door.

Don came and unlatched the screen. "It's just Pete and Jim Bob," he said over his shoulder. The boys entered.

"Sit down and cool off," Roger said. He reached under the sagging sofa cushion on which he was sitting and slowly pulled out a pistol. The sight of the gun stopped Pete as he started to sit down. Jim Bob's blue eyes grew round.

"You all scared us," Roger said. "We're not supposed to have Dad's gun. But this is his day off and he and Mom went to town, so we just thought we'd look at it."

"Oh." Pete dropped onto the chair. He knew that Roger's father worked as a guard at the Pascagoula shipyards.

Roger held out the gun. "Look at it if you want to. But be careful—it's loaded."

"Oh?" Pete gingerly took the gun. After a moment he carefully offered it, stock-first, to Jim Bob. "You want to handle it?"

Jim Bob hesitated. "Wel-l-l, if you think it's all right." He took the gun and almost dropped it. "Say, I didn't know a pistol was this heavy."

"Just keep it pointed toward the floor ... or ceiling," Roger said. "Don't point it toward anybody."

In trying to obey Roger's instructions not to point the gun toward anybody, Jim Bob ended up pointing it at everyone. Roger finally stepped behind me and cautiously took it out of his hands.

"I'd better put it away now," Roger said calmly. But his hands shook and he had turned pale. Pete folded his arms across his middle and his breath came out in a long, low whistle. Roger returned the gun to his parents' bedroom.

"Let's go out in the backyard," Pete suggested. "It's hot in here."

The four boys went out through the kitchen into a small screened porch.

"Hey, I smell cantaloupe," Jim Bob said.

"Would you like some?" Don picked up a basket filled with small melons and took it out in the backyard, where the boys sat down in the shade of a spreading live oak a short distance from the water's edge. The yard was cluttered with tin cans and other bits of trash, and some ragged chickens scratched and pecked at the bare ground.

Roger and Don took out their pocket knives—frog stickers, they called them—and began cutting the cantaloupes.

Jim Bob took a wide slice, pushed the seeds off with his finger and bit into the juicy salmon-colored fruit. "Melons are almost as good down here as they are in Oklahoma," he said enthusiastically. The chickens came and ate the seeds.

The boys were talking and laughing and eating, when a sudden splash near the bank caused them to turn around.

"Yiips! An alligator!" Jim Bob yelled as they all jumped up.

The head of the alligator rose up over the bank and the ugly reptile began moving slowly toward them. Roger, Pete and Jim Bob froze in their tracks, but Don ran toward the house.

"Don, quick, bring Dad's gun!" Roger called.

The screen door slammed as Don ran into the house, then it slammed again as he ran back out with the gun.

"Get behind me, you guys," Roger ordered "And if I miss, run for your lives."

Pete and Jim Bob and Don sprinted behind Roger, well back toward the house. The alligator kept coming and Roger just stood there spraddle-legged. By now the alligator was within spitting distance of him. Pete tried to yell "Shoot," but his throat was so dry that no sound came out.

Suddenly the gun went off—twice. The horny tail of the alligator thrashed wildly and the leathery forepaws and hindpaws clawed the ground.

"Stay back, you guys," Roger warned. "He can still kill you with that tail."

The boys kept their distance as the beast thrashed about in the dirt. By now, a crowd of women, children, and dogs had gathered at the edge of the Horvat yard. Barking and snarling, the dogs charged near but never right up to the alligator. The children screamed and cried, and the women tried to talk above the noise.

"Somebody call the police!" screamed a girl.

"I called," a woman said. "Soon as that boy hollered fer a gun. Course I didn't know he wanted to shoot a 'gator with it."

Don ran and stood by Roger, who squared his shoulders and stood firm. Pete and Jim Bob looked on.

A police car, its siren wailing, came down the street and stopped out front. Seconds later two uniformed policemen came around the house.

"What's going on here?" one of the policemen demanded. "We got a call—" Seeing the gun in Roger's hand, he stopped short. "Boy, what're you doing with that?"

Roger waved the gun toward the alligator just as the reptile raised its head in a last feeble struggle.

Instantly the policeman drew his gun. "What the—!"

"No need to waste the bullet, Dave," his companion said. "Looks like that fellow's had it—right between the eyes."

Cautiously the policemen and the four boys examined the alligator. He was very dead.

"Right between the eyes is right. Twice. And not more than an inch apart." The policeman looked at Roger.

"Just luck, I reckon." Roger looked at the ground and worried a pebble with the toe of his worn sneaker.

"Wasn't neither," Don said proudly.

"Jack, the chief'll come nearer believing this story if we show him a picture," Dave said. "Go out to the car and call for a newspaper photographer."

People and dogs crowded closer around the alligator. Roger began working his way out of the crowd. "I'd better go put Dad's gun away," he said.

"Wait till the photographer gets here," Don whispered to his brother.

They didn't have to wait long, for soon the other policeman came back around the house with a man who was carrying a camera.

The photographer studied the scene and asked a few questions. Then he said, "Okay. You four guys line up behind the critter." He began focusing his camera. "You folks in the background, step aside please."

Roger, Don, Pete, and Jim Bob in that order stood alongside the alligator. Roger stooped and placed the gun on the animal's side just behind his front leg. The flash from the camera went off in their faces, blinding them for a moment. Then the reporter jotted down names and a few details for his story.

"Now we gotta measure this baby," the reporter said as he handed one end of a steel tape to Roger. They measured the reptile at seven feet and three inches.

"Wow!" Jim Bob exclaimed. And the crowd began babbling again.

The policemen and the reporter turned to go, then the reporter turned back, saying, "Watch the newspaper tomorrow, boys."

"We will," Jim Bob promised. He was bouncing around as excitedly as if he himself had shot the alligator and were writing the story, Pete thought.

"And incidentally, don't try to carry that critter off anyplace." The policeman laughed and winked.

Roger poked at the huge lifeless body with his toe. "I reckon Dad'll have to rent a winch truck so's we can take him off in the country somewhere and skin him. We can sell his hide and throw the rest of him in a bayou for the other alligators to eat."

"Ugh!" Jim Bob's lip curled back.

Later, at home, Pete and Jim Bob had trouble convincing Pete's mother that a full-grown alligator had come up out of Back Bay.

But Grandpa chuckled. "I don't know, Kasamira," he said "When you and Peter were young'uns, wasn't nothing at all for a 'gator to come up out of Back Bay. Course it doesn't often happen anymore."

The next day Pete watched for the newsboy and grabbed the newspaper before it hit the front steps. He ripped off the rubber band and unfolded the paper. There on the front page was a three-column-wide picture of himself and his friends standing behind the alligator. The moss-draped oak and the waters of Back Bay were in the background.

"Hey, Mom! Grandpa! Look!" Pete tore through the house and into the kitchen, where he spread out the newspaper for his family to see.

" 'Youth Shoots Alligator in Yard.' " Mom read the headline.

"How about that!" Grandpa beamed.

"You guys read it later. I want to show it to ole Jim Bob," Pete babbled, gathering up the newspaper.

"Don't you think *ole* Jim Bob has a paper of his own?" Mom asked.

"Yes, but I want to show him anyhow." Pete ran out the back door and toward Jim Bob's house.

The boys met halfway between their homes and, standing where they met, read the story aloud, each from his own newspaper. When they finished reading they mauled each other joyously, and then Jim Bob became serious.

"You know, Pete, I'll bet that alligator wasn't after us at all."

"Oh? He sure had me convinced."

"He did me too, at the time," Jim Bob admitted. "But you remember, those overripe cantaloupes really smelled loud. It could've been that he was just after them."

"Maybe you're right. I never thought of that."

Captain Pete

HURRICANE WEATHER

One afternoon in late July, Pete left his bicycle near the carport and went to his room to put away his bank book. He was almost as proud of the little red book as he was of the eleven dollars recorded in it. The account wasn't as large as he would like it to be. He had spent over four dollars on presents for his sisters' sixth birthday and he had bought himself a western shirt. He hadn't really needed the shirt—and it was too hot to wear it right now—but the instant he had seen it in the store window he had wanted it.

Proudly he took the shirt from the drawer and looked at it. It was tan with red piping on the collar, cuffs, and buttoned-down pocket tabs. A cowboy riding a horse and roping a calf was embroidered in green, red, and blue on the back. Pete carefully folded it and put it back in the dresser drawer. He put his bank book in the drawer and went back outside, where he found Lala and Lenka in the hammock. Pete straddled the swing board and rocked back and forth against the ropes.

"It sure is hot and sticky," Lenka said.

"Hey, look what I've got." Jim Bob called from a distance as he hurried across the yard. His voice sounded different.

"What?" the twins asked, sitting up in the hammock.

Jim Bob curled his lips back and pointed toward his teeth.

"Braces!" cried the twins.

"They don't help my looks right now," Jim Bob said. "But maybe someday they will."

"You know what?" Lala said. "Someday when your teeth get all straight, you're going to be handsome."

Jim Bob's tan took on a pinkish cast and he fumbled with his notebook.

"What's new in your notebook?" Pete asked. "Abigail," Jim Bob answered.

"Abigail? Who's that?" Lenka asked.

"Abigail the hurricane," Jim Bob explained. "She's over on the other side of Cuba right now and she's not very big yet, but that doesn't mean she won't get big or that she won't visit us."

"You're not really afraid of hurricanes, are you?" Pete asked.

"I sure am," Jim Bob admitted. "And Mother and Daddy are scared stiff of them too."

"You mean you people who've lived in Oklahoma all your lives and had tornadoes every year ..." Pete could scarcely believe what Jim Bob was saying. "Man, I'll take my chances with a hurricane any day before I will a tornado."

"Not me," Jim Bob said emphatically. "It's like Mother says. You can go into a hole in the ground and get away from a tornado But if you go into a hole in the ground to get away from a hurricane, you'll be drowned."

"But what if you don't have a hole to go into?" Lala asked.

"They have lots of storm cellars in western Oklahoma," Jim Bob said.

"I wouldn't worry too much about it," Pete said. "We don't have near as many hurricanes in Mississippi as they do tornadoes in Oklahoma."

During the next few days Jim Bob carefully logged Hurricane Abigail's movements. He talked about the storm so much that one night as Pete lay in bed listening to the rain and wind outside his window he wondered if he could keep a written record of the storm, or of anything else for that matter, as well as Jim Bob was doing. The very question in his mind made him ill at ease. Some of his lowest grades in school had been on written assignments. He had to admit that he probably couldn't do as well as Jim Bob was doing. As if to shut out some voice, he jerked the sheet up over his head. But it was no use; the voice was inside. *Maybe you do need more schooling*, it said. He thought, Maybe if I went to summer school next year and the next I could catch up with Jim Bob. "Bah!" Throwing the sheet back, Pete flopped over on his stomach and went to sleep.

Although Hurricane Abigail was still far out to sea, the Gulf area began getting strong gales and tides two to three feet higher than normal. Heavy rains fell all one morning and the wind whipped everything in its path. Right after lunch Mrs. McElroy and Jim Bob came over to the Razettas'.

When they were inside the kitchen, fumbling with the buttons on their raincoats, Mrs. McElroy said, "Mrs. Razetta, I know you think we're silly, but Herb is in Jackson on a business trip and James Robert and I simply don't know how to cope with a hurricane." Her blue eyes were wide with fright and her hands shook as she pushed her wet, blond hair out of her face.

Captain Pete

"You probably aren't half as frightened as we would be of a tornado," Mom said understandingly. "But really, we aren't going to have a hurricane. The twelve o'clock news said the storm had already spent itself, and the rain and wind should be over by night."

In his bedroom, Pete stood with Jim Bob at the window and watched the storm. A big pecan tree just outside the window stood stiff and rigid against the wind. Suddenly a limb broke off the tree and crashed to the ground. Across the street, three slender longleaf pines bowed low. Watching them sway, Pete quietly said to himself, "Sometimes you have to bend with the wind to keep from being broken."

Lala burst into the room. "Come on, you guys, Mother made us some fudge. Let's go."

In the kitchen, the children ate fudge while Mom and Mrs. McElroy and Grandpa drank coffee. Pete and Jim Bob played game after game of checkers, with Grandpa kibitzing. Pete prided himself on being good at checkers, but he had to stay constantly on guard, for Jim Bob was good at it too. Pete won by only one game and Grandpa said he wouldn't have come out that well if Jim Bob hadn't been so scared of the storm.

Mrs. McElroy and Jim Bob stood at the picture window looking out. "We really ought to go home," she said slowly. "It's almost time for supper."

"That won't be necessary," Mom said. "Since your husband's out of town, why don't you spend the night with us?"

"Would it be terribly inconvenient for you?" Mrs. McElroy asked.

"Of course not. The boys can have the studio couch and you can have Pete's bed."

Pete and Jim Bob smiled at each other and Mrs. McElroy sighed. "Oh, thank you. I was really dreading for James Robert and myself to have to spend the night alone."

Mom and Mrs. McElroy began preparing supper.

"Captain Zett didn't take tourists to the island today, did he?" asked Mrs. McElroy in a worried voice.

"Oh, no!" Mom answered. "He never takes tourists out when the water's as rough as it's been today. He'll be home soon."

The rain and wind stopped during the night and the sun came up bright and clear the next morning.

In less than two weeks, Jim Bob was keeping notes on another hurricane. This one was named Beulah, and Jim Bob said it was "battering the boats" over in the Bahamas.

It didn't last long. But the tourist trade had dropped off with the beginning of the hurricane season and in one week Dad had allowed Pete and Jim Bob to spend two days on Ship Island. Jim Bob was able to finish his research and write his mystery story, and one hot August afternoon he read the whole thing to Pete and Radmilla. In the story a pirate, burying his treasure chest on Ship Island, dug up a human skeleton. The pirate was so scared that he ran away, leaving the chest of gold sitting out in the open.

"Well, what do you think of it?" the young writer asked when he had finished reading the story.

"Wel-l-l, it's fair," Radmilla said slowly.

"It's corny," Pete said flatly.

Jim Bob didn't seem discouraged as he sat tapping his braces with his pencil. "Well," he said thoughtfully, "I've heard that all good stories have to be rewritten several times. But I thought this one was pretty good." After a moment he asked, "What's wrong with it?"

Radmilla looked at Pete.

Pete said, "Jim Bob, it'd take more than a skeleton to scare a pirate away from his treasure chest."

Captain Pete

Even so, Jim Bob's story had made an impression on Pete and that night he had a horrifying dream. A peg-legged pirate was chasing him on Ship Island and Pete was running for his life until he fell and broke his leg. The black-bearded pirate was stooping over him and reaching out with huge hands when, trying to scream, Pete woke himself up. He was wound up in his sheet and wet with sweat. One leg was twisted under him in such a way that it had gone to sleep. He untangled himself and rubbed the circulation back into his leg.

It was some time before he was able to go back to sleep and when he did, he dreamed again. This time he saw an iron ring imbedded in the sand under a clump of willow trees on the windward side of Ship Island directly opposite the old lighthouse. He began clawing the sand around the iron ring with his bare hands and right there before his eyes was a chest full of gold coins and jewelry. He was gathering up great handfuls of coins and pearls and rubies when he again woke up.

Lying still and breathing hard, Pete stared wide-eyed into the night. A small, cool breeze floated through the open window and brushed his cheek. They were just dreams, he knew, but something about them made him awfully uncomfortable. Was some force trying to show him where to get money to put in his savings account for his boat? Of course not. Every foot of sand on Ship Island had been turned dozens of times. Or had it? Wasn't it just possible that some small spot had been missed?

Pete licked his dry lips, slipped out of bed, and went to get a drink. The street light on the corner shone into the kitchen. Pete stood in the doorway and drank the glass of water. He was wide awake by now; still he couldn't shake the dreams from his mind.

Suddenly he had an inspiration. Leaving his glass on the cabinet, he quietly let himself out the back door, cautiously crossed the carport, and cut across the lawn toward Jim Bob's house. A dog across the street barked and Pete crouched behind a shrub to wait for it to stop barking. His heart pounded and he breathed heavily, although the night air was cool. A thin moon hung low in the west; the eastern sky shoed the first pale light of dawn. A mockingbird began to trill at the top of the tall pine in Pete's backyard. Easing from behind the shrub, he crept on to Jim Bob's bedroom window.

"Psssst," he said, scratching the screen with his fingernail. "Jim Bob," he whispered hoarsely.

"Huh?" Jim Bob muttered and turned over.

"Shh. It's me. Pete."

The dog across the street barked again.

Jim Bob shot up on the side of his bed and leaned into the window. "What ..."

"Shh. Listen. Don't ask any questions. Just be at my house in time to go to Ship Island with Dad this morning."

"Why?" Jim Bob whispered loudly.

"Because we're going to dig for gold today."

"What!"

"Shh. I'll explain later. Just be there!" Pete turned from the window and hurried back home, quietly letting himself in and fastening the screen door behind him.

He went back to bed but not to sleep. When the first ray of sunlight shot across his bed he got up and dressed. When he went out into the carport, he let the screen door bang just a little. As he had hoped, Dad soon came outside.

"Why are you up so early, son?"

Pete went straight to the point. "Please, Dad, let Jim Bob and me go to the island today. I want to dig for gold."

Dad blinked, then his friendly, crooked grin began to spread over his face.

"Don't laugh, Dad. It's something I have to do. I had some awful dreams last night."

"I'm not laughing at you, son. I rather envy you. I just wish I were young enough to dig for gold."

"Then we can go?" Pete was so excited he could hardly breathe.

"Sure, if that's what you want to do."

"Yippee! Will we need to take shovels from home?" Pete turned toward the utility room.

"No," Dad said. "You can borrow them from the tool shed on the island."

"Then I'll go pack us a big lunch and fill the water jug and—" He bumped into Mom as he bounded in at the kitchen door.

"Hey, Mom, I have to make a lot of sandwiches and—"

Mom put up her hand. "I just heard all about it." She finished buttoning her blue robe, rubbed the sleep from her eyes, and started breakfast.

A SEARCH FOR GOLD

Pete carried the water jug and Jim Bob carried the lunch sack as they trudged across the island, each carrying his own space. They had worn sneakers and long pants to protect their feet and legs from the harsh grasses. Jim Bob had warmed to the gold-digging adventure until by now it was hard to tell which boy was more excited. They talked constantly as the midmorning sun slanted downward into their faces.

"What if we find a skeleton of one of those soldier-prisoners of the Civil War instead of gold?" Jim Bob asked.

"Well, what if we do?"

"I'm gonna run, that's what," Jim Bob said.

Pete laughed. "Why? Dead men's bones can't hurt you."

"No, but they can sure make you hurt yourself trying to get away." Jim Bob chuckled. After a moment he urged, "Now tell me that dream again. Exactly where did you see the iron ring?"

So for the dozenth time, Pete retold his dreams. By now the dreams had taken on a few curlicues and near the end of the telling of the second one, Pete suddenly interrupted himself. "Jim Bob, you've got to stop asking me to tell the dreams. You're going to make me forget just where to look."

They walked on in silence for a while. Suddenly Pete stopped and looked northward toward the old lighthouse. He

Captain Pete

scanned the whole area back toward the windward side of the island.

"The place doesn't look like it did in my dreams," he said uncertainly.

"Of course not," Jim Bob said brightly. "Dreams never tell the exact details. They just give you a hint and you have to take it from there."

"The lighthouse was there," Pete mused, "and a clump of trees was over here near the water." He could scarcely believe that the trees were not there.

"No matter," Jim Bob insisted. "Let's look for the iron ring anyway."

Carefully searching the ground, they walked in circles over small knolls and valleys formed by the drifting sand.

Feeling a bit foolish for having believed his dreams, Pete stopped abruptly and sat down. "I'm tired and hot. Let's have a drink." He unscrewed the caps from the water jug and filled the first one and handed it to Jim Bob. Then he filled and drained the second one three times.

"I wouldn't care if I had a sandwich," Jim Bob said.

"Me neither."

Each boy ate a sandwich, an apple, a handful of cookies, and a bunch of grapes.

Pete stretched out on his stomach to rest. "Ouch!" He raised up to move what he had supposed was a rock under his ribs. "Hey, Jim Bob, here it is!" He clawed at the sand with both hands.

"I told you! I told you it didn't matter about the trees!" Jim Bob jumped up and grabbed his spade.

Pete pushed his space into the ground just inches in front of Jim Bob's. "Shucks," he said, shoveling away the sand, "it's just a rusty old chain." Disappointment swept over him.

"Dig!" Jim Bob said. "The pirate might have fastened a long chain onto the chest so he could find it easier when he came back.

The boys dug frantically until they had uncovered both ends of a chain about ten feet long.

"Just a piece of an old anchor chain," Pete said in disgust. They stood looking at the large hole they had dug to follow the twisting directions of the chain.

"I give up." Jim Bob threw his space aside and stretched out on the ground on his back. He threw his arm across his eyes to shade them from the noonday sun.

Pete leaned on the handle of his spade and watched as water oozed into the hole. He had heard that if you buried an empty barrel three feet deep on the island it would soon seep full of sweet water. A chunk of wet sand caved from the side of the hole, exposing a bit of something white. Pete hopped down into the hole and scratched at the object with his finger. It was bone. He gouged deeper.

"Hey, Jim Bob. I'm finding a skull."

Jim Bo bolted to a sitting position. "You're kidding me."

"No I'm not." Using both hands, Pete dug the skull out of the bank and brushed off some of the sand. Then holding it behind me, he climbed out of the hole and started toward Jim Bob.

"Pete! Don't you dare!" Jim Bob scrambled to his feet and ran like a turkey.

Pete started laughing and Jim Bob stopped running and turned to look.

"It's a skull, all right."

"I don't believe it."

"Come look."

"No." Jim Bob kept his distance.

Captain Pete

Pete brought his hand from behind him and held out the skull. Jim Bob stretched his neck to look and walked slowly back toward Pete. "I still think you're teasing."

"Look at it," Pete said. "See. Two eye sockets and a nose."

Jim Bob came closer. "So it is. But what *kind* of a skull?"

Pete laughed. "I'd say raccoon."

"Oh, you—!" Jim Bob took the small skull in his hands. "Can I have it for a souvenir?"

"Why not?" Pete grinned. "I've had my fun with it."

The boys sat down and finished their lunch.

"I tell you, this isn't the place," Pete insisted as he screwed the caps back on the water jug. "It was on beyond the lighthouse, and there were some trees at the edge of the beach on the windward side."

"Well, I sure don't see any such trees," Jim Bob said crossly. "I'll go on with you just a little farther, and if we don't find anything soon, I'm heading back to the fort." He grabbed up his spade and swung it across his shoulder.

Pete picked up his spade and the nearly empty water jug and they walked on. The afternoon sun was hot on their bare backs. Suddenly they topped a long sandbar and there at the bottom of the draw were three small pine trees.

"There it is!" Pete shouted and ran. A clump of dense bushes grew around the pines, and as the boys neared the spot they heard a groan. They stopped and stared at each other.

"Ooooh." The moan came from beyond the underbrush.

Jim Bob's eyes widened and his braces seemed to jump out. Pete's scalp prickled.

"Eee-o-oh."

"Let's get outta here, Pete!" Jim Bob had turned a sickish green.

"No. Wait," Pete choked.

"I-o-oh. Hal-l-p!" The cries were louder and more anguished.

"Pete! It's the ghost of a pirate!" Jim Bob gasped. "I'm leaving!" He turned and headed toward the fort.

"Wait! Maybe it is a ghost, and it's calling us to where the treasure is."

Still running, Jim Bob shouted over his shoulder, "You can have your treasure."

"Eee-o-oh! You thar. Halp me!"

Pete's mouth was dry and his palms were wet as he listened to the anguished groaning. He looked quickly about. It was only a few feet to the trees; it was a mile or so back to the fort. Jim Bob had stopped at the top of the sandbar.

"Halp me!" The voice was urgent.

Pete swallowed a gulp of air and strained to see through the bushes, but the leaves were too thick. Setting the water jug down and carrying his spade point forward like a spear, he cautiously rounded the bushes. A man, lying on the ground, rose up on one elbow and glared wildly at him. Pete threw down his spade and ran.

Jim Bob stood silhouetted against the bright western sky. As Pete ran, he called, "Jim Bob! Jim Bob!" He motioned for Jim Bob to come back. Slowly Jim Bob came down off the sandbar. When they were about to meet, Pete called, "It's Old Joe Sark and he's hurt or sick or something. You have to come help me."

But the instant Pete said "Old Joe Sark," Jim Bob stopped. "Oh, no, I'm not," he said. "You're not getting me back down there. Not with him."

"Jim Bob, don't be silly," Pete scolded. "Something's wrong with him and you've got to help me."

Jim Bob shook his head and backed up. "No. I'm afraid of him."

Captain Pete

"But we can't just leave him here," Pete implored. "I think he's out of his head–and what if he hurts me?"

Apparently that was the wrong thing to say, for Jim Bob turned and ran. Pete looked after him in disbelief. Then he turned and looked back toward the trees. Again looking after Jim Bob, he called, "Jim Bob, wait. Listen to me."

Jim Bob stopped and looked back.

"If you won't come back and help me," Pete called, "then hurry to the concession stand and tell them to call the Coast Guard. They'll know what to do. Tell them exactly where we are."

"Okay. I'll do that." Jim Bob wheeled and ran. Still carrying his space, he disappeared over the sandbar.

Pete turned back toward the trees. Josiah Sark had called to the water jug and was trying to get the caps off. Pete ran to him.

"Water! Water!" the old man gasped.

Captain Pete

"Yessir, I'll give you water." With shaking hands, Pete unscrewed the caps and poured out the water. He tried to hold it for the old man, who was still lying on his stomach and propped up on his elbows. But dirty, gnarled hands grabbed the cup and spilled most of the water.

"More, boy. More" The old man trembled. His bearded face and parched lips were swollen and his black eyes were glassy.

Pete emptied the few remaining spoonful's of water into the cup and handed it to the old man, who drained it greedily and then fell forward with his face in the sand.

"Mr. Sark, what's the matter?" Pete asked, daring to turn the old man's head enough so that he could breathe easier.

"Broke my laig."

Pete looked and gasped at the sight. The man's left leg was so swollen that the laces of his boot cut into his flesh. "What happened?" Pete asked, looking around. The flattened grass and the markings in the sand indicated there had been a struggle.

For the next several minutes Pete listened while the old man told a long, rambling story about how he had gone fishing and had had motor trouble. When he had lifted the motor off the boat to try to fix it he had stumbled and dropped it, breaking his leg. He made sense part of the time, but part of the time Pete was sure he was out of his head. And through it all he kept asking for more water and Pete kept trying to tell him there wasn't any more. The old man mumbled and his voice trailed away.

Pete tried hard to think what to do. Suddenly he grabbed up his T-shirt and ran and dipped it into the salty sea water. He hurried back and began washing the old man's face.

"How long have you been here, Mr. Sark?"

"Don't know. All I recollect is it was a Monday when I come out."

"Then you've been here two days and nights," Pete said. "This is Wednesday."

"Two days ... two weeks ... dunno ..." The old man closed his eyes. Again Pete tried to think what to do. He started to get to his feet, but the old man grabbed his arm and squeezed it so hard that it hurt.

"Don't leave me," he cried.

"I won't leave you," Pete promised.

"Yes, you will. Like your friend. You'll run off and leave me."

"No. He went to get help," Pete tried to explain.

"Hal-l-p! Somebody halp me-e-e." The old man's hold on Pete's arm relaxed and Pete decided he had slipped into unconsciousness. He tried again to ease his arm away, but the gnarled, gritty fingers held him tightly. "Wa-ter!" wailed the old man.

With one hand, Pete turned the jug upside down again to show him there wasn't any more water. Suddenly he remembered the hole he and Jim Bob had dug before noon and how the water had begun to seep into it before they left. But the hole was over on the other side of the sandbar. He waited till the old man dozed, then he jerked his arm loose and jumped out of reach.

"Don't leave me, boy. We're gonna die here together. Remember? Together."

Mr. Sark, I'm not going to leave you." Pete tried hard to convince him. "I'm going to get you some water, and I'll be right back."

"Don't leave me."

"I'll be right back. And I'll bring you some water."

"You do that, boy. You bring me water. And hur-ry ..." His voice trailed away.

Captain Pete

Pete waited long enough to make sure that the old man was still breathing, then he grabbed the jug and ran to the hole. The water was already inches deep, but it wasn't very clear. Pete took a sip of it and, finding that it wasn't salty, he carefully dipped several cupfuls into the jug and then ran back to the trees.

Josiah Sark raised himself on one elbow. "Water?"

"Yessir, I brought you some water." Pete poured out a cupful and the old man gulped it down and fell back on the ground.

Pette looked about. He wanted to drag the old man back into the shade, but he was afraid to move him. He might fight, or the extra exertion might prove too much for him. Pete decided to let well enough alone.

As he waited, trying hard to be patient, Pee wondered who would rescue them, and how. It would be great, he thought, to ride in the Coast Guard cutter. He scanned the water in the direction of the coast line and strained to hear the sound of a motor. But the rolling, swishing rhythm of the waves shut out other sounds. Occasionally a flock of gulls flew by, screeching loudly.

What had happened to Jim Bob? Pete was sure he'd been gone long enough for someone to have come. But when he looked up to guess at the time of day, the sun seemed to have stopped at a little past noon. Maybe Jim Bob hadn't been gone as long as it seemed.

Pete looked at Mr. Sark's swollen leg and again he wished he dared pull the man back in the shade. He went around the clump of bushes, and the markings in the moist sand indicated that the old man had spent most of his time there. Looking up at the trees, Pete realized it would remain shady there most of the day. A short distance farther on was old Joe Sark's blood-red boat tied to a log. The motor lay nearby. "Water," the old man called, and Pete ran to him.

"Boy, you promised not to leave me."

"I didn't leave you," Pete said. "I was looking for your boat."

"You lie," the old man accused. "You been gone two days in my boat."

Pete held a cup of water for him. The old man drained the cup and said, "You're a good boy. Not like that one that stole my boat and left me here to die." He fell back onto the ground. "We're gonna die here together, boy. You and me. We're friends. … Die together …" He drifted off again and Pete moved away.

Shading his eyes with both hands, Pete stood looking toward the fort. Jim Bob and someone slightly taller than he topped the sandbar and Pete started to run to meet them. Then suddenly hearing the racketing sound of a motor, he looked up at a helicopter almost directly overhead. He shouted, waved his arms, then grabbed his T-shirt and began waving it. It had never occurred to him that he would be rescued in anything but a boat.

With its engine roaring, the helicopter hung momentarily in the air, then slowly settled to earth. Sand and bits of grass whipped up by the whirring blades stung Pete's face and the bare upper half of his body. He bowed his head into it and shouted for joy. Jim Bob ran up behind him and slapped him in the back.

"We came as fast as we could and looks like we just barely got here in time," Jim Bob gasped. His red face was streaked with dirt. "You okay?"

"Sure. What took you so long?" Pete asked.

"This is Phil Grayson," Jim Bob panted. "He was looking for adventure on the island and I told him to come with me. I didn't know but what we might need help before the rescuers came."

"Hi." Saying no more, Pete turned back toward the helicopter.

Two men had climbed out with a stretcher and were lifting Old Joe Sark onto it. "What's your name, boy?" one of them asked.

"I'm Pete Razetta and this is my friend Jim Bob—"

"You mean Captain Zett's son?" the man interrupted as he and the other one carried the stretcher toward the helicopter.

"Yessir." Pete tried to explain further, but the man said, "We'll get the details later. Got to get this man to the hospital."

Pete ran to a safe distance as the shuddering helicopter slowly rose from the ground. He and Jim Bob and Phil Grayson watched as it banked and headed back for Biloxi.

On the way back to the fort, Pete told Jim Bob and Phil everything that had happened, trying not to leave out any of the details. They reached the fort in time to board the *Clipper Catt* on its last trip back to Gulfport for the day.

The next evening, all the children from the neighborhood milled about in Pete's backyard, looking at copies of the newspaper.

Captain Pete

" 'Youths Find Injured Man on Ship Island.' " Radmilla read the headline. Pete and Jim Bob almost burst with pride as she read the story. "Pete's name appears more times than Jim Bob's," Radmilla said. "It doesn't seem quite fair. After all, going for help was just as important as staying with the man."

Jim Bob grinned. "Maybe so, but I'll have to admit that it took more courage to stay than it did to run. And boy howdy, I ran."

"Are you going back and dig for gold under those trees?" Roger asked.

"Naw," Pete answered. "The spell's broken. Besides, I don't think there's any gold out there."

"If I was Old Joe Sark," Don said, "I'd sure be glad you had them dreams. 'Cause if you hadn't he likely would've died out there."

"Oh, perish the thought," Radmilla said.

"Perish the thought is right," Pete echoed. "He really scared me—talking about us being friends and dying out there together."

Mom stepped out into the carport. "Jim Bob, your mother just called. She said for you to come home to dinner."

"Okay. Thanks, Mrs. Razetta." Folding his newspaper, Jim Bob turned to go.

"We'd better go too," Roger said to Don. The crowd broke up, leaving Pete to glow over the newspaper story alone. When Dad came home the talk resumed, this time with the family taking turns reading the reporter's colorful account of Pete's and Jim Bob's adventures.

THE SECRET AT THE BLOODY DOOR

One night after the rest of the family had gone to bed Pete sat on the floor practicing knots while Dad listened to the late news. Using a forked stick, he made a cleat hitch, then using one prong as a piling, he made a clove hitch. These were easy, but the bowline and the anchor bend were more complicated and he had to ask Dad for help.

When the weather news came on the television the reporter said hurricane Corabelle was coming toward Cuba.

"Here we go again," Pete said. "Jim Bob'll be over here first thing in the morning with his notebook."

Dad looked at Pete. "No, no. You loop it the other way for an anchor bend." Pete tried again and Dad said, "That's right." And then, "What's the matter? Don't you like the way Jim Bob reports hurricanes?"

"I just get tired of the way he carries on."

Pete was right in his prediction that his friend would come early and with notes on the latest tropical storm. Jim Bob caught him sweeping the carport.

"Ole Corabelle's sure kicking up her heels," Jim Bob began.

"It probably won't even come near here," Pete said.

Jim Bob squinted at Pete. "You sure are an optimist about hurricanes."

"I'd rather be an optimist than a pestimest," Pete said.

Captain Pete

"Well!" Jim Bob sputtered. "I don't know whether you meant to say 'pessimist' or whether you mean I'm a pest."

Not wanting to give Jim Bob the satisfaction of knowing that he'd made another mistake, Pete just grinned and kept on sweeping. Jim Bob said he had some books to return to the library and went on his way.

Grandpa enjoyed watching television, and for the next two days his programs were interrupted with news bulletins about hurricane Corabelle. By the middle of the week, the Florida Keys were being raked with winds of hurricane force. Gale warnings had been posted as far west as the Mississippi River.

"That gets us, doesn't it, Mommie?" Lenka asked when she heard the news bulletin.

"Yes, dear," Mom said brightly. But Pete thought Mom didn't look as cheerful as she tried to sound.

"I hope Daddy didn't take the *Clipper Catt* to the island today," Lala said.

"Daddy is a cautious man, dear," Mom said. "Let's not worry about him."

But the wind grew stronger and the rain came down harder. Pete began to worry about Dad and the *Catt*. By noon the temperature had dropped considerably, and Pete put on his western shirt. It was still a bit warm for a long-sleeved shirt, but he was so proud of it and he had wanted to wear it for so long. He was standing in the front door looking out when the letter carrier stopped his cart out on the street. Pete ran down the walk in the rain to meet him.

"Hi, Pete," the postman called. "Looks like you got a letter. Take it and run." He handed Pete a stack of mail then hurried back to his cart.

Glancing at the mail, Pete saw that the top letter was addressed to him in a very queer way:

TO PETE RAZETT
SON OF CAPTN ZETT

Pete ducked in out of the rain.

"Pete, did you have to do that?" Mom scolded. "Couldn't you have let the postman bring it to the door?"

Pete handed the mail to Mom, wiped his feet on the throw rug, and went to his room. He tore open the envelope addressed to him and read:

COME TO BLOODY DOOR AT ONCT
YORE FRIND
JOSIAH SARK
PS COME ALONE OR BE SORRY
COME QUIK

Pete stared at the message. It was only one week since he'd found Old Joe Sark out on the island. Could he be out of the hospital this soon? Pete wondered. Stuffing the note into his shirt pocket, he sauntered back through the house and out to the utility room where he kept his bicycle. Mom would never let him go if she knew, but could he get away without being seen? If only the twins didn't come looking for him. He put on his raincoat, eased his bicycle out the door, then jumped on it and took off. Once out into the street he split the rain like a huge yellow bird flapping along the ground.

When he reached the Back Bay area he had to slow down, for his bicycle careened and pitched on the unpaved streets like a frisky jack rabbit. When Pirate's Tree and The Bloody Door

Captain Pete

came into view he almost lost his nerve. "What am I doing here?" he asked aloud, braking to a stop. Panting hard and feeling the rain run down the back of his slicker off his rain hat, he looked about. No one seemed to be watching him. He didn't know whether that was good or bad. In a way he wished that someone knew where he was. He walked his bicycle on toward the blood-red door and leaned it against the shack. Taking a deep breath, he knocked lightly on the door.

"Who's thar?" the old man shouted from within.

Pete gave the door a little push and it swung open.

"Ah, I knowed you'd come. A friend never lets a friend down." Josiah Sark grinned, showing toothless gums. He sat in a ragged, dirty, over-stuffed chair. His left leg, in a cast from his toes to above his knee, was propped up on a box. A crutch leaned on either arm of his chair.

"Mr. Sark, I thought you'd still be in the hospital," Pete said.

"Hee, hee." The old man cackled. "I raised so much Cain they was glad to brung me home." Then in a low voice, "But they ain't found it. They ain't nobody found my secret yet. They ain't a gonna find it neither."

"Sec-cret?" Pete stammered.

"Shet the door, boy. Then set a spell." He indicated a rickety chair that he most of the back rest broken off.

Afraid not to obey, Pete closed the door, then eased down onto the edge of the chair. Puddles of water formed where the rain dripped off his slicker. "I ... I can't stay long. Nobody knows where I am."

"That's right, boy. I done told you to come alone. You done the right thing."

As the old man talked, Pete looked quickly about. The only light in the musky-smelling room came through two small windows. Nearby was a dirty, lumpy bed without sheets or pillowcases. At the other side of the room was a broken table and on it were a hot plate and some pans containing dried leftover food. The floor, if you could call it that, was made of uneven boards, some warped and broken. Walls and ceiling were covered with heavy gray paper, torn and sagging and full of dust and cobwebs. Pete had never seen such poor surroundings and he felt sorry for the old man. He'd ask Mom to bake him a cake and—

"And that's why you had to come alone," Josiah Sarak punctuated his statement by pounding the floor with a crutch.

Pete jerked upright. "Sure, I understand." That wasn't quite the truth, but it would have to do until he could think of something better. His eyes had adjusted to the dim light and he noticed that the old man's face was sallow. But his black eyes were bright and penetrating.

"I ain't never told nobody my secret, but you're my friend, so if you'll promise not to tell it I'll tell you."

Pete squirmed, not sure that he wanted to share this man's secret. "Wel-l-l, yessir, if it's something I'm supposed to know." He waited, and when the old man didn't continue, he said, "I ... I really have to go now. But I'll be back, and I'll bring you something to eat. ..."

"I got plenty o' grub!" The old man's black eyes snapped. "An' you can't go yet." He motioned for Pete to sit back down, but Pete preferred to stand—at a little distance. "I ain't told you my secret yet, boy. Now you understand I ain't gonna tell you where I keep my secret." He shook his head and gestured with his hands. "Not because I've got anything against you. No, 'tain't that atall. You and me, we're friends. But sometimes even friends don't tell everything."

"I understand," Pete said.

The old man reached over and patted the dirty mattress.

Captain Pete

"My secret's right under there and I'm gonna let you hand it to me. Course that ain't where I keep it, but that's where I put it, knowin' you'd come."

Breathing heavily, Pete hesitated, his eyes glued to the hump in the mattress.

"Go ahead, boy. Reach under there and hand it to me."

Pete slowly raised the edge of the mattress. There was a dull-green metal box, and as Pete reached for it Old Joe Sark watched him like a cat watching for a mouse to come out of a hole. Handling the box as carefully as if it contained dynamite, Pete pulled it from under the smelly mattress and set it across the old man's lap. With the thing out of his hands, he took a deep breath.

"Ah-h." The old man signed and grinned his toothless grin. "Ain't many people got what I got here. He gently stroked the box, then opened it.

Pete gasped. He'd never seen so much money in one place in all his life. Was the old man a thief? Suddenly Pete was more frightened than he'd ever been before.

"I ... I have to go," he stammered, turning for the door.

"Wait, boy! I brung you here to give you some o' this."

"Oh, no! No. I ... I can't take it."

"And why not? You saved my life."

Pete stared at the old man.

"You saved my life," he repeated. "I want to pay you for it."

"Oh, no!" Pete said. "You don't save somebody's life for money."

"I know that, boy! But the money's mine and I can do what I want with it. I been savin' it ever since I come back from France the Christmas of 1918 and found my ma and my pa dead with the flu. ..." He blinked his black eyes several times. "I saved my money, and ever time I got enough I went to the bank and had it changed to a hundert-dollar bill." He lifted the top one off and handed it to Pete. "Look at it, boy. Ain't it purty?"

Pete took the bill and turned it over. He had never seen one before. "Why didn't you put your money in the bank so it'd draw interest?"

"No, boy, no! Don't you never trust them banks. Why durin' the Depression I seed people lose every thing they had." He interrupted himself. "But you wouldn't be old enough to know about the Depression."

"I've heard Grandpa talk about it." Pete held out the hundred-dollar bill. "I won't tell your secret, Mr. Sark."

"Take that with you. It's yours. You saved my life and I want you to have it."

"But …"

"No buts about it." Mr. Sark snapped the lid shut on the battered green box.

Unable to believe what was happening, Pete just stood there.

"G'wan home afore the hurricane hits." The old man waved a crutch.

Pete shook his head. "I can't take—"

"Put it in your pocket and git," Old Joe Sark ordered. "Yer ma's likely standin' on her head about you already."

As Pete hesitated, the old man whacked the metal bedpost with a crutch. "Git!"

"Yessir!" Pete jerked open the blood-red door and gasped as the cold rain hit him in the face. He turned back. "Thank you, sir."

"Git!"

Pete jumped out into the rain, slamming the door behind him. With trembling hands, he unbuttoned his raincoat and stuffed the bill into the left pocket of his cowboy shirt, making sure the tab was buttoned down.

Gullies of muddy water ran down the street and Pete had to walk his bicycle up the hill to where the paving began. It took him longer to return home than it had taken him to reach The Bloody Door. He panted hard, but no more from exertion than from excitement. And he dreaded facing his mother. His sneakers were covered with mud. He remembered seeing a clean pair on top of the drier in the utility room, and he hoped he could change before Mom caught him. But as he rounded the corner into the carport he bumped into Dad.

"Pete, haven't you got better sense than to be out in weather like this?" Dad scolded. "Where've you been? Your mother's worried about you."

But before Pete could answer, Dad continued, "Put that bicycle away and help me with the windows."

"Do you really think we'll have a hurricane?" Pete asked, wheeling his bicycle into the utility room, behind Dad.

"It certainly looks that way," Dad answered. "There's no point in taking chances. Here, help me with this plywood. We'll cover the picture window just in case, but I think tape will do on the others."

Captain Pete

TAPING UP AND BUTTONING DOWN

"You boys be careful," Mom called from the kitchen door as Pete and Dad started across the carport with the large sheet of plywood. "Sometimes I think more people get hurt taping up and buttoning down for a hurricane than from the storm itself."

Just then the wind jerked Pete's end of the board out of his hands and slammed Dad backward against the station wagon. Pete grabbed the board again and they wrestled with it around the house and until Dad had it secured to the window frame with nails. As they worked, Pete searched for a chance to tell Dad about Old Joe Sark and the money. But the wind was so high and the rain was so blinding that there was no time for talk. He kept touching his shirt pocket to make sure the money was still there.

Mom had supper waiting when they finished taping the windows, and at the table before all the family didn't seem the place to discuss the money.

"Kasamira," Dad said, cutting a bite of steak, "do we have plenty of flashlight batteries and candles in case of a power failure?"

"Yes, I think so. And plenty of canned goods." Mo wrinkled her forehead. "It might be better if we had a few more loaves of bread."

Everything they had done so far was routine for a hurricane warning. Dad and Mom and Grandpa began talking about the bad storms they'd had in the past. Pete didn't become uneasy until they told about one that had washed out long sections of sea wall and demolished many boats. Pete asked, "Do you think this one will be that bad?"

"You never can tell about a hurricane," Dad said. "It can be coming straight at you and you can pack up to run, then suddenly it can turn and take off in the opposite direction and you won't even have to go."

"Oh, that reminds me," Mom said. "Mrs. McElroy called to say they were going to a hotel, just in case the storm should move in during the night."

"Good," Dad said. "They'd probably panic if it did."

Lala said, "The Horvats came by with their car loaded full of things and they said they were going to spend the night with friends out in the country."

Dad looked at Mom, and Mom nodded.

"Pete, don't wolf your food so," Mom scolded gently.

Pete hadn't realized his nervousness showed.

Suddenly Dad pushed back from the able. "I'm going to put out more lines on the *Catt*."

"I'll go help." Pete gulped the last of his glass of milk.

"Oh, Pete," Mom cried.

"It'll be rough," Dad warned.

"I want to help," Pete pleaded. The wind nearly knocked Pete down as he and Dad fought their way to the car.

Cautiously driving through the blinding rain, Dad stopped near the door of a grocery store. He pressed some money into Pete's hand and told him to get six large loaves of bread.

Pete jumped out of the car and sprinted inside the store. The grocer had only three loaves of bread left. Most of the shelves were empty of canned goods. Pete paid the man and ran back to the car.

The windshield wipers were almost useless against the rain, and the twisting wind rocked the car as they drove along.

Pete felt the money in his shirt pocket. "Dad, I never did tell you where I was when you came home this afternoon."

"That's right. You didn't."

"I was down at The Bloody Door and Old Joe Sark gave me a hundred-dollar bill," Pete blurted out.

"What!" Dad slowed the car.

"He said I saved his life and he wrote me a letter and he gave me a hundred dollars." There. It was all out and Pete felt better.

"Now wait just a minute." Dad glanced quickly at Pete. "Back up to the beginning, boy, and take it a little slower and give me a chance to understand what you're saying. I thought Old Joe Sark was in the hospital."

"He was, but he said he raise so much Cain that they were glad to take him home."

"*That* I can believe," Dad said. "But what did you say about a hundred dollars?"

"Dad, it was the biggest boxful of money I ever saw—"

"The beginning! Please!"

So, beginning with the letter carrier and the crude note Pete told Dad the whole story, trying to include all the details. "He wouldn't take the money back, so I put it in my shirt pocket."

"Do you mean to tell me that you've got a hundred-dollar bill in your shirt pocket now?" Dad asked.

"Yessir. But I'd sure like for you to take it. At least till we get back home." Pete unbuttoned the pocket tab and took out the money.

"Well, for the time being it's just as safe with you as it would be with me," Dad said. "Put it back in your pocket."

"What if I lose it?"

"Then you'll be right back where you were before you got it." Dad turned off the highway and drove down to the harbor, where all the small craft were bucking like broncs at a rodeo.

"I think the rubrail will keep the *Catt* from dashing too hard against the dock," Dad said. "Pete, that wind's awfully strong. Do you think you can make it down the pier?"

"Yes. But we might better crawl on our hands and knees."

"I think you're right. And we might just as well leave these slickers in the car." Dad struggled out of his. "We'll be soaked anyhow, and they'd only catch the wind and get in our way."

Slipping out of his slicker, Pete took a deep breath and jumped out into the cold rain. The zigzagging wind slapped him against the car, then sucked him away from it. He felt his shirt pocket to make sure the tab was securely buttoned.

"Pete!" Dad shouted above the howling storm. "You'd better stay in the car."

"No, I can make it!"

"Then you go first. So I can keep an eye on you."

Pete dropped to his knees, then crawled and slid on his stomach down the long wet pier. He turned left where the dock formed a T at the end of the pier, and when he reached the *Catt* he clutched the rail and pulled himself over onto the deck. Dad was right behind him. The *Catt* pitched so that they were tossed back and forth between the rail and the benches. When they reached the stairway leading to the upper deck, each dragged out a coil of rope from underneath it and Dad turned to the bow and Pete turned to the stern.

The boat tossed and Pete plunged headlong, skidding both elbows on the slippery deck. He staggered to his feet, only to be thrown sideways into the benches. Getting up again, he threw the rope over his shoulder and grabbed the rail with both hands. When the boat bumped against the dock again, he sprang overboard. Fighting to stay on his feet, he slipped a clove hitch

Captain Pete

over the piling, then jumped back on deck to secure the other end of the line to the boat.

"Give her plenty of slack so she won't break a line!" Dad shouted from the bow.

"Aye, sir!" When Pete opened his mouth to shout back, the wind and rain almost took his breath away.

Dad staggered sternward and examined the line Pete had put out. "You did a good job, mate," he said. "Let's go before we're blown away." Just then the lights went out and Pete and Dad clutched at each other. The harbor and the city of Gulfport were in darkness; the only lights in sight were the car lights along the highway.

"Climb over the rail, Pete, then get down and feel your way," Dad said.

Pete obeyed, and down the length of the pier Dad kept hold of one of Pete's ankles. When they reached solid ground they got to their feet, clinging to each other. Dad gathered Pete under his arm as they staggered toward the car. They were running their hands along the side of the car in search of the door handle when the lights suddenly came back on.

"It was just a a temporary power failure," Dad explained.

On the way home Pete said. "This is a pretty bad hurricane, isn't it, Dad?"

"No, we don't have hurricane winds yet," Dad answered.

"Then what does it take to make hurricane winds?" Pete asked in astonishment.

"About seventy-four miles an hour. It's hard to judge what we're getting, but I'm sure it's not that much yet." Dad had tried the car radio, but the static was so bad that they couldn't understand anything on it.

"Dad, I aim to give Jim Bob half of this money," Pete said abruptly, "but what'll I do with the rest of it?"

"Do whatever you want to with it. It's yours."

Captain Pete

"I could put the whole fifty dollars in my savings account."

"Why not? You'll still have your mowing for spending money."

"Yippee!" Pete yelled and pounded Dad's shoulder.

Dad grabbed Pete's wet leg and squeezed hard. "Looks like you're going to have a big down payment for a boat long before you finish junior high school."

Mom met them at the kitchen door. "Dear me!" she exclaimed when she saw how wet they were.

"Our slickers didn't do us much good." Pete was so cold his teeth chattered. Puddles of water formed on the floor around him and Dad.

"You'd better get hot showers so you won't take colds," Mom said.

Pete headed for the bathroom. Then he turned aside to his room and spread the wet greenback out on his dresser to dry. The front of his beautiful cowboy shirt was ruined; all muddy and snagged from the rough boards on the pier. He looked at it sadly, then put it on a hanger to dry. If Jim Bob was keeping a raccoon skull for a souvenir, he guessed he could keep a shirt.

The noise of the storm grew louder as the increasing winds drove torrents of rain slanting across the windows and slammed debris against the house. Something hit the plywood shutter over the picture window, causing Pete to jump straight up out of his chair. Grandpa disconnected the television set, but he kept the transistor radio turned on for news of the storm. Mom put candles, matches, and flashlights on the coffee table and then sat down on the divan with one arm around Lala and the other around Lenka. When the twins finally fell asleep, Dad and Mom carried them to their beds.

Captain Pete

Pete curled up on the divan, determined not to sleep, but he must have dozed in spite of himself, for when a loud noise brought him upright he yelled, "Where's the lights?"

"Just stay where you are," Mom said. She turned on a flashlight and then lit some candles.

Dad tried the telephone and found it out of order. Pete went from window to window, peering through the crisscrossed tapes, but as far as he could tell the whole city of Biloxi was in darkness. The kitchen clock had stopped at 11:57. Dad wound his wrist watch to make sure it didn't stop during the night.

Dad, Mom, Grandpa, and Pete listened intently to the broken voice coming over the radio. There had been a power failure all along the Gulf Coast and no promise could be made as to when power would be restored.

"Unconfirmed reports say that a section of sea wall has been washed out near Gulfport," the newscaster said, "but we don't have the exact location. A motorboat has been washed across Highway 90 west of Biloxi."

"Dad, do you think it got the *Clipper Catt*?" Pete asked anxiously.

"I don't think so, son. We put out some strong lines." Dad's words were reassuring, but he continued pacing the floor.

It was well past two A.M. when the wind and rain began to let up a little. Sometime later, Pete lay down across his bed, still determined not to sleep.

At first Pete thought the electricity had come back on. Then he realized it was daylight. He jumped up and ran into the kitchen. He found Mom out in the carport.

"Where's Dad?" Pete asked.

"He left at daybreak to see about the boat," Mom explained.

"Oh, Mom," Pete wailed. "I wanted to go with him."

"I doubt that he would've let you. He said there'd be lots of cleanup work to do and maybe some rescue work and that there was no telling when he'd get back home."

It was still rainy and gusty. Lawns and streets were covered with a soggy carpet of leaves, green pecans, pine cones, and here and there a large tree limb.

Over near Jim Bob's, Pete saw a large uprooted tree lying across the street. A metal road sign was twisted around a water hydrant. Picking his way through the debris, Pete went around the house. Other families were out in the rain surveying the damage to their homes. Most of the men had gone to the major disaster areas to help with the cleanup work. Pete went in at the front door and found Grandpa listening to the transistor radio.

"Lots of damage reported in the Biloxi and Gulfport harbors," Grandpa said. "Five boats have been washed ashore here in Biloxi."

"Oh, Grandpa!"

"Tides are ten to twelve feet higher than normal," Grandpa continued.

Pete gasped. He ran through the house and out to the utility room for his bike.

"Mom, may I go see the high water?" he asked, straddling his bicycle.

Mom looked at him for a long moment, then as if she understood she said. "Yes. But do be careful, and don't be gone too long."

Pete pedaled down the street and around the fallen tree. Once over the crest of the hill, he could see the high water, ugly and dirty and churning with debris. A houseboat was smashed against a live oak tree at the shoreline. Pete turned at the next street corner and went as fast as he could go among the rubble toward The Bloody Door.

Captain Pete

He stopped at the top of the hill and looked down to Pirate's Tree; the water swirled high above the knothole where Jean Lafitte had left his love notes. The Bloody Door was gone! With rain spattering in his face and goose flesh rising on his wet, bare arms, Pete stared, mouth open. The angry water lapped at the eaves of the houses that still stood along the shore.

A man in wading boots was poking around in the muddy water with a fishing pole. Pete walked his bicycle toward the man and called, "Sir, do you know Old Joe Sark?"

The man looked up. "Yes, I know him."

Pete hesitated, almost afraid to ask, "What happened to him?"

The man sloshed out of the water. "His brother came over from Pascagoula last night and him and me carried the old coot out bodily."

"Did he ... take ... any of his things?"

"*Things?*" the man echoed. "What things? I didn't see anything in that pest hole worth taking. Not even him."

Pete gulped. How was he going to find out ...?

"No, sonny, he didn't take anything. Nothing but a little old green battered metal box. Hung onto it like it was his very soul—"

Having heard what he wanted to hear, Pete turned abruptly and headed back up the hill.

"Hey, there, boy," the man called. "Why did you ask?"

Pete pretended not to hear. He jumped astride his bicycle and took off. He was well away from the place before his legs or his heart slowed down.

He decided to go by the Horvat house, where he found the water up to the window sills. He was glad the Horvats had taken refuge in the country. Pete turned home. Pedaling across the backyard, he let his bicycle fall on the lawn and he burst in at the kitchen door. "Mom!" he cried. "The water! It's way up in some of the homes. In the Horvats' …"

"I know," Mom said sadly. "Your father and I were down there early this morning." She put milk, dry cereal, and fruit on the table. "Come eat your breakfast," she said, paying no attention to Pete's wet clothing.

The twins and Grandpa were seated at the table. Pete glanced up at the kitchen clock; the hands still stood at 11:57. Mom looked at her wrist watch and said, "It's ten forty-five"

"Has Dad called?" Pete asked.

"The phone's still dead," Lala said.

"Grandpa, what about the *Catt*?" Pete asked

"We'll just have to wait and see, Little Pete," Grandpa said.

Mom laid her hand on Pete's shoulder. "We're fortunate, son," she said quietly. "Even if we've lost the boat, we still have our home and our lives. And that's enough to be thankful for. Eat your breakfast."

But as Pete ate, he knew that life would never be the same if they had lost the *Clipper Catt*. Not even if Dad bought a bigger and better boat.

There was a knock at the front door and Pete ran to answer it. It was Jim Bob.

"Didn't I tell you ole Corabelle'd give us trouble!" Jim Bob said. "We just stopped to let you know we're home."

"Come in," Pete said, holding the door open. "And tell your Mom and Dad to come in too. I've got something to tell you. Hey, Mom," Pete called toward the kitchen. "It's the McElroys and I asked them in."

Pete hurried to his room and got the hundred-dollar bill. When he returned to the living room, his family and the McElroys were gathering there.

Captain Pete

"You'll never believe it," Pete began. "Just look what Old Joe Sark gave me yesterday!" He held up the bill.

"What!" Jim Bob's blue eyes seemed to jump out of their sockets—just the way Pete knew they would.

"Where did you get that?" the twins wanted to know.

"Shh," Mom said. "You'll hear the whole story. Go ahead, Pete."

Pete tried to begin at the beginning, but so much had happened since late yesterday afternoon that his brain was like a tilt-a-whirl in high gear.

"Old Joe Sark warned me never to tell his secret," Pete said, frowning, "but how was I going to give you half of this without telling you where it came from?"

"Half!" Jim Bob cried.

"Oh, no," Mrs. McElroy said quickly. "James Robert couldn't possibly take that much."

"I couldn't?" Jim Bob said, his braces showing.

"No, you couldn't," Mr. McElroy said. "You ran. Pete was the one who stayed."

"Twenty-five?" Jim bob asked.

"No. Ten," his father said.

Wait just a minute," Mom said. "This whole thing is between the boys. I think they are the ones who should decide."

"Twenty?" Jim Bob looked at his parents.

"Ten," his mother said quietly.

"Oh, no, ma'am," Pete said. "He must take at least twenty."

"Lenka, bring my purse," Mom said. "I have a twenty-dollar bill that we'll give to Jim Bob right now and Pete can pay me back."

With that settled, the two families discussed Old Joe Sark and his box of money.

"I still hate that I had to break my promise not to tell," Pete said, and Mom said, "Well, the important thing is that we not talk about it any more than we have to."

"That's right," Mr. McElroy agreed. "If the wrong people should learn that the old man has money, no doubt somebody would do him bodily harm to get it."

"That's what keeps scaring the daylights out of me," Pete admitted.

"Well, with his shack washed away and him at his brother's home," Mom said, "no harm should come to him."

"Let me see that," Jim Bob reached for the hundred-dollar bill. "And everybody thought he was a pauper."

"Ain't that a honey." Pete handed over the bill. "You reckon old Benjamin Franklin ever figured his picture would be on something like that?"

"James Robert," Mrs. McElroy said, worrying her blond hair, "it looks like you're going to get your portable typewriter sooner than you'd expected."

Jim Bob handed the hundred-dollar bill back to Pete. "Looks to me like you're going to get the money for your boat sooner than you thought, too, Pete."

ADVICE FROM SAM TATE

That afternoon, when the rain had stopped, Pete and Jim Bob went exploring along he flooded shore.

"There are two things we have to look out for," Pete cautioned. "Water moccasins and live electric lines. Be sure you don't step on or touch a wire—no matter what."

The water had receded several feet since morning, leaving soggy heaps of seaweed, dead fish and snakes, ships' cargo and household furnishings.

The National Guard had been called out and the uniformed men, working in pairs, were walking along the shoreline shooting snakes or standing guard near damaged buildings to prevent looting. Deserted houses stood gaunt and washed out, their gaping black windows reminding Pete of the empty eye sockets in a skull. The boys walked on unmindful of the time. As they came around the corner of a large building, the setting sun shot a golden beam at them across the Mississippi Sound.

"Hey, Jim Bob, we'd better turn back," Pee exclaimed. "It's getting late and we're a long way from home."

It was dark before they reached home, but fortunately the electricity had been restored and the street lights had come on. As Pete entered the carport he saw Mom in the kitchen fixing supper.

"Mom," he called, taking off his muddy boots and leaving them outside, "have you heard from Dad?"

"No." Mom sounded very upset.

Pete stepped inside the kitchen.

"We've had the radio on all days," Grandpa said. "But we haven't heard anything about the small-craft harbor at Gulfport."

After supper, Grandpa and the twins went to bed, but Mom and Pete waited up for Dad. It was nearly midnight when he came home. Pete ran out to meet him.

"Dad, what about the *Catt*?"

"She's all right, son." Dad clamped a firm hand on Pete's shoulder.

Mom held the screen door open and Dad stepped inside and dropped wearily onto a chair. Pete dropped to his knees and began taking Dad's muddy boots off his feet.

"Biloxi was much harder hit than Gulfport," Dad began. "But once I was in Gulfport I couldn't seem to get away. There's lots of cleanup work to be done there."

Clad only in his pajamas, Grandpa spoke from the doorway. "They said on the radio that at least five boats have been washed ashore here around Biloxi."

"Yes," Dad said. "Wonder if they belong to anyone we know."

"I haven't heard," Grandpa said.

"Several boats were damaged in the Gulfport harbor," Dad said, "but only one was washed ashore. I don't believe any loss of life has been reported."

"Not that I've heard," Grandpa said.

"This will just about end the tourist season, won't it, Zett?" Mom asked.

"I'm afraid so. Most of the tourists left ahead of the hurricane," Dad said, "and now with the opening of school not far away, people are winding up their vacations and getting back home."

Captain Pete

Suddenly Pete's old problem was back to haunt him. What should he do about school? He knew that if he would really buckle down to it, he could make better grades. But who wanted to study that hard? He could play hooky day after day and eventually just quit. But what would Grandpa think of him then? Four more years just to finish junior high school! He left the others in the kitchen talking about the storm damage and went to his room and looked at his bank book.

The next morning Pete begged to go to Gulfport, but Dad said no. "Your mother needs you here. All that mess in the yard has to be raked up and put in boxes so it can be hauled off. Then you must mow the lawn."

So Pete stayed home and raked the yard, making mounds of leaves and tree limbs. Mom came to inspect the work while Pete went to Brown's Grocery Store for empty boxes. He found Sam Tate out behind the store leaning on his broom.

"Hi, Pete," Sam greeted him. "You 'bout ready for school?"

"Not exactly," Pete replied.

"Well, it's just around the corner, you know. I figured you and me'd be thinking right strong about it. At night I'll be there pushin' a broom"—Sam gave a little demonstration with the broom in his hands—"while you're home with your nose in a book. And during the day when you're at school with your nose in a book I'll be home asleep." Sam chuckled.

"I know," Pete sighed. "But right now I need some boxes."

"Help yourself."

Pete fished several cardboard boxes out of the trash bin and fitted the smaller ones into the larger ones.

"You know, Pete," Sam said, still leaning on his broom, "I wish you could find it in your heart to like school a little better."

"Why?"

Sam kicked a pebble and sent it bouncing across the ground. "You see, Pete, when I was your age I didn't like school either. And in them days there wasn't no law to make parents send a kid to school if he didn't want to go. Leastwise I never heard of one. So I quit school when I was twelve years old, not knowin' much more than how to read and write."

Sam rubbed his chin. "When the war started, my rich uncle—Uncle Sam, that is—sent me on a all-expense paid trip over Europe that lasted for years. Then I come home and got married ... It was then that I realized I'd wasted some mighty important years." He looked at Pete soberly. "Get you a education, Pete. You ain't got no choice this day an' time but to get you a education."

Remembering how Grandpa had talked to him the first day they had taken Jim Bob to Ship Island, Pete asked, "Have you been talking to my grandpa?"

"Nope. Why?"

"I just wondered. Thanks for the boxes."

"Take all you want," Sam said elaborately. "Just saves them other fellers from havin' to haul 'em off."

Pete turned the stack of boxes upside down over his head and went thoughtfully home.

Shortly after the hurricane people began coming down with a strange new virus. Within a few days the hospitals were filled to overflowing. The ailment lasted only a day or so, but while it lasted, the patient was violently ill for hours at a time. The McElroys had all been sick at the same time, and Pete had run errands for them and his mother had cared for them and cooked their meals.

Dad had continued to go to Gulfport each day, then one morning he said, "For two cents I wouldn't even go to the dock today. I haven't had a load of tourists since the hurricane and it's just a waste of time to go down there and stand around."

Mom looked at him understandingly.

Dad poured himself another cup of coffee, took one swallow of it, and left the table. In a moment he was back with his cap in his hand.

"Change your mind?" Mom asked.

"Habit, I guess." He kissed Mom and left.

Grandpa had scarcely spoken during breakfast. But as soon as Dad left he slowly got up from the table. "Kasamira, I think I'll go back to bed. I'm afraid I've got one of those viruses they keep talking about."

"Papa, you certainly don't look like you feel well," Mom said. "Let Pete and me help you."

Pete jumped up and put one arm around Grandpa's waist. The frail body inside the light summer robe leaned against him. It was a small thing, but it stirred strange feelings in Pete. His grandfather had always been a source of strength to him and suddenly it seemed that their positions were reversed. It gave Pete a sobering sense of responsibility.

"Grandpa, you're going to be all right," Pete said as he and Mom helped him to the bed.

Grandpa didn't speak. As he lay back on his pillow his jaw slackened and the pallor of his face frightened Pete.

"Grandpa?" Pete said anxiously.

"I just don't feel like talking, Little Pete," Grandpa said wearily.

Mom called the doctor at nine o'clock and sent Pete to the drugstore for the prescription which the doctor phoned in. Just before noon Grandpa grew violently ill and Mom began trying to locate Dad by telephone. She called the harbor at Gulfport and the man told her that the *Clipper Catt* wasn't at her berth.

Hanging up the telephone, Mom said thoughtfully, "Even if Zett had a load of tourists this morning he should be back by now."

"Mommie, can't you make the doctor come see Grandpa?" Lenka cried.

"Honey, he had to go to the hospital," Mom explained. "I guess he can't get away."

Pete stayed by Grandpa's bedside most of the day, giving him the medicine as prescribed. Around four o'clock in the afternoon Grandpa began to feel better; then later, while Mom cooked dinner, he insisted on sitting in an armchair near the kitchen door so he could feel the cool breeze.

Pete stood with his arm around Grandpa's shoulder. "I'm glad you're feeling better, Grandpa. You sure had us worried there for a while."

"I tell you, boy, them viruses can sure make a body sick." Grandpa's voice sort of squeaked. "But the doctor's little pills have got a powerful wallop. They knocked that bug in the head in a hurry."

Mom turned from the kitchen sink. "I really don't think you should've gotten up yet, Papa."

"But, Kasamira, it's such a long day when you're flat on your back," Grandpa said.

When Dad came home, well after sundown, he took one look at Grandpa and exclaimed, "Papa, what's wrong?" He listened with a worried look on his face as the rest of the family related the incidents of the day. "I heard some of the fellows over in Gulfport talking about their families having that stuff too."

"But, Zett, where were you all day?" Mom asked.

"Me? Oh." Dad smiled. "This morning I helped Jake and Wade work on their boat. Then around eleven o'clock a family came—a man and his wife and three teenage boys—wanting to go to the island. I told them I couldn't make the trip for five people, but they were s set on it that we settled for thirty-five dollars. They had a basket lunch with them, and I didn't have anything else to do, so I just stayed out there till they got ready to come back."

"Was there much damage on the island?" Grandpa asked.

"Almost no damage," Dad said sitting down to the late dinner Mom had kept warm for him. "Lot of stuff washed ashore, but that can all be cleaned up."

The next morning, Pete was awakened by the ringing telephone. He heard Dad get out of bed o answer it.

"Hello?" Dad said. "What's that again? ... Oh? ... Why, yes, I remember ... No, no. Just a reasonable day's wage will be fine ... Yes, I'll go right away."

It was a strange conversation, and Pete slipped out of bed and went into the hall to listen.

Dad wrote down a telephone number then repeated it back into the phone. "I'll call you as soon as I know." He hung up the receiver.

"What was that all about?" Mom asked; she had come to listen too.

"That family I took out to the island yesterday," Dad said. "The man lost a billfold someplace and he wants me to go back out to Ship Island and see if I can find it."

"Where is the family now?" Pete asked.

"In Mobile," Dad answered. "They drove on over there yesterday evening. He said they'd wait there for my call and if I found the billfold they'd come back for it.

"I'll hurry with breakfast," Mom said.

"Dad, I'll go with you," Pete said.

"Okay."

Dad and Pete dressed, ate breakfast, and left.

BACK TO SHIP ISLAND

The harbor was quiet when Pete and Dad loosed the *Catt's* moorings and put out for Ship Island. Proudly standing beside Dad, Pete said, "Captain Zett, I guess this makes me your first mate, doesn't it?"

Grinning faintly, Dad laid a hand on Pete's shoulder. Pete looked up at his father, hoping that he would let him take the wheel.

They had gone only a short distance when Dad said, "I've got the craziest feeling, Pete. Like I'm seasick."

"Seasick!" Scarcely believing his ears, Pete looked at his father again. "Dad, you can't be seasick! But you do look pale. What'd you eat for breakfast?"

"Not much of anything, in case you didn't notice," Dad said. "For some reason, I just didn't feel like eating this morning."

They'd gone on in silence for some time when Pete asked, "Did that man tell you what his billfold looked like?"

"Yes. He said it was bright red plastic. Said it contained his credit cards and some very important papers." Suddenly Dad folded his arms across his stomach. "Take the wheel, Pete. I'm sick."

Pete grabbed the wheel and steadied the boat. "Dad, I've never seen you sick," he said in bewilderment.

Captain Pete

"And I can't remember when I've ever been sick. But I'm sick now and we shouldn't have started out by ourselves this way."

Pete knew what Dad meant, and he knew that he was right; they really were undermanned. And what if Dad should get as sick as Grandpa did yesterday? For over a year Pete had been begging Dad to let him manage the *Catt* all by himself. Now the sudden realization that he might have to frightened him. He said, "I can manage the mooring lines when we get there."

"The way I'm feeling, you might have to manage more than that," Dad said. "I know it sounds crazy, but I'm hot and cold at the same time. If you'll get that pillow and blanket out of the bunk I'll lie down awhile."

Dad took the wheel and Pete quickly lifted the padded lid of the bunk and got the pillow and blanket, then he took the wheel back.

"The water's rough this morning, so you'll have to be careful," Dad said, settling himself on the bunk. "I won't go to sleep but call me if you run into any trouble."

"Aye, aye, sir."

As Pete stood alone, gripping the wheel with both hands and fighting the rough sea, a feeling of responsibility swept over him with such violence that he trembled. What if he should meet other boats? Would he remember the rules? He went over them in his mind: In case he should meet another boat, he had to pass to starboard and blow one short blast on the whistle. In case he was about to cross the path of another vessel, he had to stay clear if the other boat was on his starboard side. He shook his head and thought hard. "If they come in on my left, they have to keep clear," he told himself. "If they come in on my right I have to keep clear." He groaned, almost hoping he wouldn't meet anyone.

As if reading Pete's thoughts, Dad asked, "Is everything all right, mate?"

"Yes, sir. We're right in the middle of the channel and no other craft's in sight."

"Fine. Just hold it on ten knots."

Pete knew that Dad held the *Catt* on nine knots when taking tourists to the island—that timed it just right so that he could make two trips a day. Sighting on a distant buoy, he held the wheel firmly and battled the surging waves. Eventually he allowed his body to relax a little.

Dad had been quiet for some time and Pete turned and looked at him. The blanket had slipped to the floor. Pete left the helm only long enough to snatch up the blanket and put it back over Dad, but when he returned to the wheel he'd lost his sighting on the buoy. He was more than halfway across the sound by now and the sea had grown rougher. He grasped the wheel and struggled with it until he brought the boat back in line with the buoy.

Although Pete knew they had been not more than thirty minutes from the island when he had left the wheel to cover Dad, it seemed hours before they began nearing the dock.

"Dad," he called anxiously.

Dad sat up quickly on the side of the bunk. "Pete! Why didn't you tell me we were this close?" He stood and swayed dangerously. "I must have dozed. You should've called me earlier."

But Pete was proud that he had been able to bring the *Catt* all the way to the island. "How do you feel?" he asked.

"Rotten." Dad laid his hand on Pete's shoulder. It was hot with fever. "You'd better get down below."

Hurrying to the lower deck, Pete picked up the bow line and as Dad eased alongside the dock he cast it around a piling and took up the slack. Then he ran for the stern line.

Captain Pete

Dad came down and checked the moorings. "You did a good job, mate." He groaned and pressed his stomach hard with both hands.

Dad leaned heavily on Pete as they stepped off the boat onto the pier. Pete asked, "Where do you think we'll be most likely to find that billfold?"

"Who knows? They were all over the island yesterday ... Wait, Pete. I've got to sit down." Dad had turned pale and he dropped to the pier."

Confused and frightened, Pete asked, "Dad, are you all right?" He knew it was a foolish question.

"No, I'm not all right," Dad answered. "But maybe this will pass if I'll just be still a minute."

As Pete stood looking down at his father, a flash of red color beyond the edge of the pier caught his eye. He leaned over and looked closer. "Dad! There's the billfold."

"What?" Dad raised his head. "Where?"

"Right down there." Pete pointed straight down. The water was still cloudy from the storm, but the sunlight picked up the bright color of the billfold.

Dad staggered to his feet and tried to look where Pete was pointing, but he nearly fell off the pier. Pete grabbed him and helped him to sit back down. "I wonder how it got there?" Dad said weakly.

"Maybe the man was carrying it in his breast coat pocket and maybe he took off his coat and it fell out."

"Maybe you're right."

"Look, Dad, you stay right here and don't let that thing get out of your sight. The water's pretty deep, so I'll run and get a rope and tie it around me and around a piling and that way I can pull myself back up."

Dad just grinned wanly.

Captain Pete

When Pete returned with the rope, Dad said, "There's nobody here but us. Why don't you take off your clothes so you won't have to go home wet?"

"Say, I'm glad you thought of that." Pete slipped out of his clothes and tied the rope around his waist.

"Be careful," Dad said.

Pete dived into the water. It was deeper than he'd expected and he had to kick hard to reach bottom. Baby conches that had been nibbling at the red plastic darted into their shells. Pete clutched the billfold, pushed it under the rope around his waist, surfaced, and then started pulling himself up, hand over hand. As he reached for the edge of the pier, the billfold slipped from under the rope and splashed back into the water. He had to go down again. This time he held the billfold between his teeth.

When he pulled himself back up onto the pier he was startled to find that Dad had disappeared.

"Dad!" Frantically he searched the water on both sides of the pier. Dad was nowhere in sight.

Dropping the billfold on the pier, Pete stood on it with first one foot and then the other as he hurriedly dressed. With shirt unbuttoned, rope over one arm, shoes in one hand and billfold in the other, Pete ran to the *Clipper Catt*. He scurried up to the pilot house and found Dad doubled up on the bunk.

"Dad!" Pete cried, shaking his father.

"Ooh!" Dad groaned, pressing his stomach hard with both arms.

Looking wildly about, Pete wondered what he should do. One thing was certain: he had to get Dad home as fast as possible. He studied the boat's controls.

"Start the motor," he told himself aloud, "then put it in reverse and back very carefully away from the pier." His hand was on the switch when he suddenly remembered that he hadn't loosed the moorings. He ran below, pulled in the lines, then ran back up to the pilot house.

"Dad! Dad!" Again he shook his father. But Dad only sighed heavily.

Back at the helm, Pete took a deep breath, started the motor, and very carefully backed the *Clipper Catt* away from the dock. Then he turned her about and headed into the channel.

PETE RESCUES THE "CLIPPER CATT"

When Pete had the *Clipper Catt* well centered in the channel he tied the wheel and went back and straightened Dad's legs and covered him with the blanket. The August sun was hot, but Dad was shivering. Returning to the wheel, Pete was startled to find that he had tied it slightly to the left; the *Catt* had crossed the channel and was headed into a buoy.

Quickly he untied the wheel and got back on course. Then he considered his predicament. On the way out, Dad had said to hold the *Catt* on ten knots. But now Pete eased her up to twelve knots. The tide was against him and the sea was even rougher than it had been when they came out. The waves broke three to five feet high, and the more he fought the wheel the more the boat rocked. He glanced over his shoulder and saw that Dad was about to be pitched off the bunk. Dad didn't wake up and Pete knew that he had lost consciousness.

Fear choked him and sweat popped out all over his body. The *Catt* was getting out of hand and Pete was so scared that for a moment he thought he was going to be sick. "Dad! Help!" he called loudly. His tongue felt as if it had needles in it. "Da-ad!" he yelled. Dad didn't answer and Pete didn't know whether he was just unconscious or whether he had died. "Dad! Don't die!" he cried.

Captain Pete

Suddenly he reduced his speed, and when the *Catt* stopped rocking and he again had her under control he eased back up to ten knots and held it there. His arms ached with the constant battle with the waves, and the silvery brightness reflecting off the water burned his eyes. Desperately he hoped that he would soon meet the Coast Guard, or some boat, so that he could ask for help.

Gradually his terror subsided, but the twisting, gnawing sensation continued in his stomach. He knew it was partly due to hunger and partly because of the excitement of handling the *Clipper Catt* all by himself. But it was also because of fear. Fear that he might do something wrong, and fear for their safety.

Gripping the wheel, he fought to keep the boat on course. In spite of the strong tide, Pete chanced a look over his shoulder. He saw the slow rise and fall of the blanket over Dad and knew that his father was still breathing. He tried to relax and think of something pleasant.

"Boy, if Jim Bob could see me now." A smile touched his face. Jim Bob had never learned to sway with the boat. "He's out of step and out of time," Pete said, "and he'll never get the hang of sailing till he learns to sway with it instead of fighting against it."

Glancing starboard, Pete saw a string of barges. "Dad!" he called over his shoulder. Dad didn't respond. Pete knew that the barges were so far away that he couldn't expect help from them. He squared his shoulders and tried to make his trembling knees behave.

It seemed hours before he approached the small-craft harbor. The Coast Guard cutter *Point Estero* was not at her station. "Must have had an emergency call," Pete said to himself. He looked about. Two men whom he didn't recognize were sitting in a car near the *Catt's* berth. Their presence made him even more nervous.

Captain Pete

"Well, Pete, ole boy, you've been bragging to Jim Bob that you could dock this thing all by yourself." He hardened his jaw. "Now do it!" he commanded. He reversed the engine and slowly eased the *Catt* into her berth.

The two men jumped out of the car and ran down the pier. "Where's Captain Zett?" one of them called.

"He's sick! Can you help me?" Pete called back.

The men jumped aboard and grabbed the lines, and when they had moored the *Catt* they hurried up to the pilot house. "What happened?" they asked.

"He suddenly got awfully sick and passed out," Pete said.

"Don't tell me Captain Zett's got the flu bug," one of the men said.

"Looks more like the bug's got the Captain," the other one said.

They shook Dad and talked to him until he groaned and began to move. Then they got him up on his feet and carried, more than walked, him off the boat. One of them said, "I'll drive him home in his car, Jake. You follow in your car so we can get back."

At home, Pete ran ahead and opened the screen door. The two men jumped out of the cars, and with Dad between them they took him into the house.

"What on earth?" Mom cried.

"Seems like you've got two captains on your hands, Mrs. Razetta," one of the men said. "This little one here had to bring the *Catt* in by himself."

"What?" Mom exclaimed.

Asking questions but not waiting for answers, Grandpa and the twins followed the others to the bedroom.

"I reckon this young captain can explain it all," the man said as they stretched Dad out on the bed. "We were just about ready to go out on a job, ma'am; will you be able to manage?"

"Yes," Mom said. "I'll call the doctor immediately." She ran to the telephone.

Pete fell onto a chair near Dad's bedside.

"Little Pete, what happened?" Grandpa asked.

"Yes, what happened?" the twins babbled.

"The Doctor'll come as soon as possible," Mom said, hurrying back into the bedroom. "Pete, can't you speak? I have to know everything so I can explain to the doctor."

"I haven't had a chance to speak yet," Pete cried. "Dad's just got the virus like everyone's had. He just passed out."

"Water," Dad groaned, breathing heavily through his mouth.

Lala and Lenka bumped into each other as they ran to the kitchen. They returned with two glasses of water. Dad drank both of them then fell back on his pillow.

"Zett." Mom gently shook Dad. He groaned and rubbed his face. "A wet washcloth," Mom said, and the twins sprinted to the bathroom and brought two. Mom took Lala's and Lala ran and got another one. While Mom bathed Dad's face the twins took off Dad's shoes and bathed his feet. Dad was ticklish on the bottoms of his feet, and sick though he was, he wiggled them and tried to get them away from the girls.

Pete tried to explain everything that had happened since he and Dad had left home early that morning.

"Zett," Mom called.

"Ooh," Dad groaned. "Where am I?" He opened his eyes wide.

"Daddy, Daddy!" the twins cried.

Dad suddenly sat up in bed. "Pete!" he called wildly.

"I'm right here, Dad." Pete jumped up and grabbed one of Dad's thrashing arms. "It's all right."

"Oh, son." Dad held Pete tightly in his arms. "I thought you'd drowned."

The family looked at each other and Grandpa said, "He's been out of his head all this time."

"How'd I get home?" Dad asked, pushing Pete away and looking at him wide-eyed.

"Jake and Wade brought you," Mom explained. "But they had to go back."

"Jake and Wade?" Dad said in astonishment. "What time is it?"

"It's noon," Mom said.

"Noon!" Dad sat upright.

Mom looked at Pete, then back at Dad. "What's the last thing you remember, Zett?"

Dad rubbed his face, then reached out and took hold of Pete's knee. "The last thing I remember, this guy was stark naked and diving into deep water. How'd we get back to port, mate?"

"I brought the *Catt* in, Captain Zett," he said proudly. After a moment he rose to leave the room. As he passed Grandpa he squeezed Grandpa's arm and said, "We made it, Skipper Pete."

Pete went out through the carport, sat down in the shade of the house, and leaned against the wall. Crossing his arms on his knees, he rested his head on them and closed his eyes. He hadn't been there long when he heard footsteps.

"Hey, Pete," Jim Bob called. "Where've you been?"

Pete raised his head as Jim Bob hurried up and dropped to the ground in front of him. "Boy, you've been wanting to write a good story. I lived one this morning. Only you'll never believe it."

"Tell me about it," Jim Bob urged.

A car door slammed out front and Pete jumped up. "That's the doctor. Dad's real sick and I want to go hear what he says about him."

"Really?" Jim Bob followed Pete to the kitchen door.

With the screen between them, Pete said, "I'll tell you all about it later, but I want to hear what the doctor says."

He hurried to Dad's bedroom and found the doctor looking into Dad's eyes with a small flashlight. Then the doctor thumped and tapped Dad's chest. Removing his stethoscope from around his neck he said, "Wouldn't you know that a big healthy ox like Captain Zett would be the very one who'd be the hardest hit by this bug? But he's over the worst of it now." Straightening things around, he snapped his bag shut. "Just give him plenty of liquids, Mrs. Razetta, and he'll be all right by morning."

Pete breathed a sigh of relief and went back outside to visit with Jim Bob.

As in other years, the Razettas had a picnic in their backyard on Labor Day. Grandpa and Grandma Bozavic and all the Bozavic and Razetta aunts, uncles, and cousins were there and also the Nincics and Horvats and Popovics. Although Dad had recovered from his ordeal, everyone made a fuss over him.

Pete, too, got plenty of attention and he had to watch himself to keep from strutting about like a puffin. All the kinfolks and friends were calling him "Captain Pete" and praising him for the fine way he'd managed the *Clipper Catt*. And somehow word had gotten out about the money Old Joe Sark had given Pete.

Pete and Radmilla were swinging in the live oak tree. "Pete, I knew you could handle the boat if you ever got a chance," Radmilla said. "But what are you going to do with all that money?"

"Dad and I have talked that over," Pete said. "I'll just leave it in my savings account to draw interest. I'm going to study real hard and maybe I can catch up with Jim Bob. And as soon as I finish junior high I'm going to buy me a motorboat."

"Wonderful," Radmilla said.

Pete thought maybe it wasn't time yet to say that he also planned to go on to the maritime academy. Grandpa had said once that each generation must improve, and now Pete knew that Grandpa had meant not only the boat but also the man, especially the man.

Teasingly he said to Radmilla, "I just might paint my boat blood-red."

"Don't you dare!" Radmilla cried.

About the Author

B. HOLLAND HECK was really Bessie Holland Heck, known to readers of the Millie Holliway stories. In this, her second book for boys, Mrs. Heck's deep familiarity with the way of life of a little-known and very colorful area of the United States adds special interest to the story. A freelance writer since 1946 and the mother of five children, Mrs. Heck lived in Tulsa, Oklahoma, with her husband.

About the Artist

ROBERT CASSELL, who for ten years operated an art studio on a riverboat on the Mississippi River, was a resident of Weston, Connecticut, where he lived with his wife and three daughters. Mr. Cassell taught at Washington University in St. Louis and has illustrated numerous books, magazine stories, and magazine articles.

Captain Pete

Epilogue

P eter Martin Skrmetta, who affectionately became known as "Captain Pete", was a European immigrant from the island of Brač, Croatia. Pete led a storied and adventurous life. In 1903 at the age of sixteen, he left the island village of Bobovišće for America. Upon his eventual arrival in Biloxi, he went to work crewing on a utility sailing schooner used to catch shrimp and freight oysters on the Mississippi Sound. This "Biloxi Schooner" model was very comparable in

Captain Peter Martin Skrmetta circa 1950

design to similarly purposed fishing vessels plying the Adriatic. So, given his experience and work ethic, he quickly became the skipper for one of the local vessel owners.

Following the technological advances driven by World War I, schooner owners began transitioning to engine power in an effort to increase their profit margins on shrimp and oyster

Ship Island Snack Bar and Fort Massachusetts circa 1946

harvesting. As a result of these improvements, Pete earned enough extra money by just 1923 to build his own 56-foot, diesel powered fishing vessel which he named the "Pan American". Ever the entrepreneur, he always looked for additional revenues and began using the Pan American for summer excursions into the Mississippi Sound. In 1926, he began ferrying passengers to the offshore barrier islands. As Pete's excursion boat business grew in popularity, he would eventually focus entirely on transporting passengers to the offshore islands.

Captain Pete

In 1933, the Gulfport American Legion leased the western part Ship Island and opened a fishing resort next to the abandoned Civil War era relict-Fort Massachusetts. The Legion immediately realized that tourists need a means to access the newly opened resort, so they offered Pete rights to transport customers from Biloxi to Ship Island. Pete accepted the offer and over the remainder of his life would provide exclusive ferry service to thousands of visitors to the island. The excursion service prospered under his direction. Eventually he would build a second passenger vessel, the Pan American Clipper, in 1937.

Following a hurricane in 1947, Pete took over management of the on-shore resort built by the American Legion and immediately upgraded the facilities. Pete had a ready-made workforce to accomplish this task. Namely, he had seven daughters, two sons plus numerous grandchildren and relatives

The Pan American Clipper in 1966

that crewed on the boats, helped operate the island snack bar, and managed the beach service. As a practical matter, family members lived on Ship Island during the summer tourist season. Life on a Mississippi barrier island sounds alluring but is always challenging. Summer heat and humidity can be brutal. Many amenities readily available in the mainland were notably absent. Nonetheless, the islands are enchanting. After the last tour boat left the island, the fun began for the kids.

Fishing, swimming in clear green island water, shelling, exploring and playing in the old brick fort was their reward for hard work. Moreover, the night sky is glorious! For the next twenty-five years Ship Island became a way of life for the Skrmetta family and is now being shared with a fourth generation. Bessie Holland Heck captures part of this life in her 1967 novel, "Captain Pete". The story is based on a young Skrmetta's Ship Island experiences.

Following Captain Pete's passing in 1963, the company was handed down to his sons - Peter Matthew and James Noel. That same year the two brothers launched the Pan American II and added a second departure point from the city of Gulfport twelve miles to the west of Biloxi.

In 1971, Ship Island and the other Mississippi barrier islands became a part of Gulf Islands National Seashore. With their years of experience and purpose-built fleet, the Skrmetta's company became the successful bidder on the first park service ferry contract. Since then, the family has been awarded several additional contracts and continues to operate the ferries and island food service as they have for over three generations.

Captain Pete

Captain Peter Matthew Skrmetta and sons Steven, Matthew, Ken, and Louis – standing in front of the Pan American Clipper during her rebuild in 1984.

2026 marks the 100-year anniversary of the Skrmetta family ferry service on the Mississippi Gulf Coast. Captain Pete's Adriatic spirit and appreciation of the American dream remains alive and well and will continue to live on through the fourth generation of Skrmetta's.

Visit our Website: https://msshipisland.com

Made in the USA
Columbia, SC
03 June 2025